Summer of Tess

Also by Dennis McKay

Novels:
Fallow's Field (2007)
Once Upon Wisconsin (2009)
A Boy From Bethesda (2013)
The Shaman and the Stranger (2015)
The Accidental Philanderer (2015)
A Girl From Bethesda (2017)

Nonfiction:
Terrapin Tales, with coauthor Scott McBrien (2016)

Summer of TESS

DENNIS MCKAY

iUniverse®

SUMMER OF TESS

iUniverse books may be ordered through booksellers or by contacting:

iUniverse
1663 Liberty Drive
Bloomington, IN 47403
www.iuniverse.com
1-800-Authors (1-800-288-4677)

ISBN: 978-1-5320-3835-8 (sc)
ISBN: 978-1-5320-3834-1 (e)

Library of Congress Control Number: 2017918504

Print information available on the last page.

iUniverse rev. date: 01/15/2018

Chapter 1

TESS AND STACY

August 1978

Not only was Tess making good money for the cross-country trip with Stacy, but she had asked Teddy, the bartender, to join them. She had not consulted Stacy about it beforehand and instead gave her the news at the waitress station as they prepared for the dinner crowd.

"When did this happen?" Stacy said as she began unloading a tray of clean glasses onto a shelf.

"Yesterday."

"I thought this was *our* last stand, the Tess-and-Stacy road trip, with diplomas in hip pocket, before getting real jobs, paying rent, and all the other BS."

"But his VW bus has so much more room, Stace." Tess was standing next to Stacy, filling a drawer with utensils. She liked the way they could work together in close quarters and never get in each other's space. "And besides, I feel safer with a guy along."

"Hah. I could kick his roly-poly ass, Tess. Come on," Stacy said as she wiped a wet spot clinging to the rim of a glass.

"You sound just like Tony," Tess said.

Though there had been a general understanding that the road trip—which had progressed over the course of the spring semester from "Wouldn't it be fun" to "We should do it" to "We must go no matter what"—would be just the two of them, Tess liked the idea of having Teddy on board, as he was easygoing and smart in that preppy sort of way and could offer a third-person voice of reason. Tess feared Stacy, her best friend since they were roommates freshman year at the University of Maryland, would throw some divergent route into the plan, which was to first head to Denver to see Tess's boyfriend, Buddy, who she had convinced herself she was desperate to visit.

The turning point occurred back in April. The trip by then a forgone conclusion, both girls were on the lookout for better-paying summer jobs to finance it. While in the student union cafeteria, Tess noticed a maintenance man at the summer employment bulletin board packing a plastic sleeve with flyers. From her corner table, Tess had an unimpeded view of the large, stylish fonts on the letterhead: Hiring Top-Dollar Waitresses.

Tess deserted her half-eaten tuna salad on whole wheat and pulled a flyer. She read it twice. *Perfect.*

She looked around to see if anyone was watching and then plunged her hand into the sleeve, gripped the entire ream of flyers, and crammed it in her book bag. The ruthlessness of this out-of-character act gave Tess a pang of guilt before she decided it was them or her. She decided on *her.*

After her last class, Tess returned to her standard-issue dorm room, containing two desks—one of which Stacy was studying at—an identical pair of steel-framed beds, bookshelves, and a closet.

"How does a summer job at a Long Island resort sound?" Tess said with a victory smile. "Perhaps a hoity-toity inn in the Hamptons." She removed the pilfered flyers from her book bag.

Stacy leaned forward, eyes scanning. "Top-dollar waitresses? Where did those come from?"

"I smuggled them," Tess said, smacking the flyers as if they were a fat wad of money, "on a commando raid at the Student Union."

"*Girl ...*" Stacy said, "you gone outlaw on me."

Tess peeled off a flyer and then dumped the remainder in the trash basket. She gave Stacy a look. *Can you believe I did this?*

"Let me read to you the description of our summer home of employment," Tess said as she sat on the edge of her bed. "'Nestled in the back pocket of a stand of tall pines overlooking a secluded cove in Southampton ...'" Tess arched an inquiring eyebrow toward Stacy, who nodded for her to continue. "'Formerly a Gatsby-style mansion, with a stone-and-clapboard exterior, wrought iron trim and pitched dormer roof, the Crockford Inn presents to the selective eye old-fashioned charm and understated class.'"

"How did you get us into this?"

"I called the phone number," Tess said as she scrolled her fingers across the bottom of the sheet, offering a false smile like a game show model, "and told the owner of the tavern that we had been waitresses since junior high—which is true. And I said we had been waiting tables at country clubs for the past two summers." Tess offered a little shrug— Stacy had worked at a diner. "Half-true. Anyway, Mr. Santini said he liked the idea of college graduates."

"Santini?" Stacy said, her eyes twinkling disbelief.

"Tony Santini—"

"Tony Santini," Stacy said, her voice almost a scream, "sounds like a trapeze artist for Ringling Brothers." Stacy had that look that Tess had come to know: mirth spilling out of eyes opened wide and working in conjunction with a lopsided smile. "Ladies and gentlemen, now presenting ... ta-dah ... the amazing Santini."

Tess squinted at Stacy. *Are you done?* "His voice was pure Brooklyn, a lot of *de's* and *da's*." She cleared her throat and changed her expression back to game show hostess. "And *lastly,*" she said, "my dear Stacy, we are the proud employees of the Crockford Inn Tavern."

The morning after Tess told Stacy that Teddy was on board for the trip, she asked Stacy if she was okay with it.

"Yeah, yeah, I'm fine with Teddy boy," Stacy said. They were filling the drawers with utensils and folding and stacking starched napkins at the waitress station.

Their attention was diverted by the *whoosh* of the kitchen doors swinging open. Tony entered in a rush, with his big-guy bustle and consumption of space that indicated he was in charge. He was carrying a case of liquor, and he clinked the contents atop the U-shaped bar.

The first time he had laid a case down so roughly Tess reacted with a look of surprise. "No sissy bottles in my joint," Tony had said with a crooked grin. How he had yet to break a bottle was a mystery to Tess.

"Ladies," Tony said, "how my girls doin'?" Tony was pure Flatbush

Italian: dark features and slicked-backed hair, thinning and receding as though in unified action; hands that were constantly in motion when he talked—and he was rarely silent; and an outgoing big-guy personality that bordered on pushy. According to Teddy, rumor had it that Tony had won the tavern in a poker game the previous summer from the scion of old Southampton money.

"Hah," Tony said in a gleeful, challenging tone as he ripped open the box with a pocketknife, "another day at the salt mines for me and my girls." As though to emphasize the point, he thumped his fist on the grainy oak bar that had been dinged and dented over the years but had maintained a glossy, tough durability.

He folded the blade, slipped the knife back in his pocket, and looked over at Tess and Stacy, an *isn't this great* expression coming over his face. He then slid a look toward the dining room, nodding in affirmation of his prized possession awash in nautical, clubby ambience, with a finished crossbeam ceiling, miniature schooners and whaling boats in glass cases, and copper lantern sconces mounted to the oak-plank walls, all in direct contrast with the owner, Tony Santini.

Tess considered Tony a walking, talking paradox in this land of blue bloods. A round peg trying to fit in a square hole. She noticed this the first day she and Stacy arrived at the inn. Tony was standing in front of the porte cochere, waving his hand frantically for them to pull in under the slate-roofed structure. His pressed and creased slacks and starched white shirt could not hide the fact that he looked out of place—Little Italy invading the Crockford Inn, which really did look like something out of *The Great Gatsby*. It was as big and beautiful as advertised, the stone-and-clapboard exterior in perfect symmetry and so many charming touches like the ivy trellises on both sides of the double-door vestibule entrance. The tavern entrance was off to the side, covered by a vertically planked, recessed oak door with a transom and arched stone lintel. Above the door was a horizontal sign with gold lettering: The Crockford Tavern. The tavern was distinguishable from the inn by its sea-green clapboard exterior complemented by a row of double-hung sash windows.

When Tess had greeted Tony as Mr. Santini, he raised his hands, palms out, his expression dramatically pained. "Please—Tony—call me

Tony," he said as his attention was diverted by a middle-aged couple exiting the front door to the inn. The man, with a shelf of rippled hair perfectly in place, was dressed in a gingham shirt open at the neck and a blue blazer with embroidered family crest; the woman, wearing a beige cashmere sweater and dark slacks, held a leather handbag by the strap in the crook of her elbow. Tony threw them a big smile and a hello nod. The woman did not acknowledge the gesture, and the man squinted a look of appraisal before they slipped into the back seat of a limousine parked along the curb. Worlds were colliding.

And so began the final summer of Tess's youth, a very fine summer to this point and with more to come, she thought as Tony emptied the remaining contents of the carton before going behind the bar.

"What do you girls got—three more weeks?" Tony said this without taking his eyes off his task at hand, grabbing a bottle by the neck and storing it under the bar, one after another.

"Here we go," Stacy whispered to Tess. "Yes, Tony," Stacy said with a rise in her voice.

Tony held a bottle in his hand, looking it over as if considering. "So, what you girls gonna do when Stacy's rattletrap breaks down in the middle of nowhere?"

The car in question was Stacy's dinged and dented 1967 Corvair, which Stacy referred to as the *Green Hornet*. Tess and Stacy exchanged a look, and Stacy lifted her chin to Tess, indicating it was her turn.

Tess said, "Teddy is coming, and we're going in his VW bus."

Tony stored the last bottle of whiskey under the bar and stood ever so slowly. He turned and faced the girls with a mocking look of disbelief. "That law school sissy." He paused like an actor on cue and then made a face as if he had eaten something sour. "And," he said with a scolding wag of his finger, "that mellow yellow bucket of bolts isn't any better, and if you break down in"—Tony flickered his fingers in the air over his head—"oh, I don't know, let's say Nebraska, where you gonna find someone to fix a Krautmobile?"

"I know a little something about cars," Stacy said. She was a tall, athletic-looking girl, and fearless she was—a quality that Tess admired. And also, she was no-nonsense and capable—changed the spark plugs and oil filters on her car, was a whiz on a sewing machine, and once decked a guy in a bar with a right hook after he placed his hand in the wrong place. Standing a hair over six feet, she had a well-proportioned body from years of competitive swimming. And in symmetry to her long body was a long face with a prominent sweep of cheekbones, a sometimes-pouty mouth that registered her mood with a twist of the lips, and wide-set dark blue eyes, bold eyes, that transmitted an attitude that said, *Whatever.*

And her fearless *whatever* stare was honed in on Tony, who said with a dismissive wave of the hand, "Youse two got a lot to learn."

It was a typical weekday lunch crowd, with one exception. A group of large, beefy men dressed to the nines, a couple of them wearing gaudy, double-breasted, pin-striped suits, came in and went directly to the bar. These were Tony's paisanos from the old neighborhood who dropped by every now and then. They wore their hair slicked back à la Tony, and with monikers like Little Al, Fat Sally, and Benny Squint, they were an affable but tight-knit collection of characters. Tess wondered if they always dressed like this—or was coming to Tony's place in Southampton a special occasion?

Standing shoulder to shoulder, foot on the brass rail, they studied the *Daily Racing Form*, kibitzing in secretive murmurs before shuffling one at a time over to the pay phone in the restrooms hallway to place bets with their bookies. All the while, their dark faces gave away nothing: a glance here, a glance there at a busboy disappearing into the kitchen, a muted ripple of laughter from the dining room, the exhausted sound of the front door opening.

Stacy had mentioned to Tess that she found the paisanos interesting in a dark sort of way. But gambling seemed their only passion, at least in the Crockford Inn Tavern, where they were big tippers and courteous gentlemen.

When one of the men, Tess could never keep their names straight, returned from his phone call, her gaze lingered for a moment on his attire: dark blue suit, pink tie, and folded pocket-square handkerchief in his breast pocket, above which was a cotton-dotted white flower lapel pin. Only the paisanos could wear a costume like that and get away with it. He narrowed his eyes to half-mast and nodded hello over to Tess awaiting a drink order. *Oh yes*, Tess thought as she returned a polite smile. *Benny Squint.*

Stacy came up next to Tess and placed a tray of empty glasses on the bar. She began to speak and then paused for a beat, recalibrating. "You wanna go out tonight?" Tess had always felt a bit uncomfortable doing the Southampton bar scene since she was in a relationship, albeit long distance, with Buddy, who was employed as a sales rep for a sporting goods company and wanted Tess to move out to Denver with him. But she wasn't ready to make such a commitment, and deep down she had doubts about whether or not he was the man she wanted to spend the rest of her life with. Why that was she could not specify; it was more a vague uncertainty. He was a nice-looking, low-maintenance guy, but there was something inside her that seemed to be looking for something more. And what that something was she did not know. Tess had thought about talking it over with Stacy but held back, not wanting to reveal her uncertainty to her best friend—at least not yet.

Even so, Tess tried not to encourage the pickup artists at the local bars who hit on her with "You're a dead ringer for Ali McGraw" or another one who told her she reminded him of Pocahontas. "What?" Tess had said.

And he replied without missing a beat, "Take me to your wigwam."

It had been an interesting summer so far for Tess, working at the Crockford, sharing a bedroom with Stacy in the private quarters upstairs, mornings at the beach, work until ten, and partying late nights at the bars. Tess was in a comfortable little groove until …

Chapter 2

THE ICEMAN COMETH

Toward the end of the lunch rush, Stacy glanced at the dwindling crowd in the dining room. "Favor, Tess."

"Uh huh," Tess said, folding linen napkins in an intricate diagonal fold that Tony had taught the girls their first day on the job.

"Green Hornet has the hiccups. Can you cover for me while I drive it to the shop?"

After Stacy left, a man came up to the empty bar and stood at the corner nearest Tess. There was something compelling and dangerous about him, from his rakish good looks to an icy, cool distance in his gaze.

Tess figured he was one of Tony's paisanos from the old neighborhood, but he wasn't dressed or built like the rest of the heavyset Brooklyn cronies in their flashy suits; instead he wore a pale blue Hawaiian shirt, with yellow floral print, that showed off his tanned, muscular arms. On his left forearm was a tattoo of a stripper in a g-string, leg wrapped around a pole. And while the paisanos looked about with an air of casual indifference, this man had the look of a soldier on patrol, his eyes darting about the room.

He looked over at Tess stacking the folded napkins, and she had the sudden notion that a magnetic force was drawing her spirit out of her body. And in that notion was a sense that it was all going to be different from here on out.

"Diamond fold, right, kiddo?" He lifted his chin toward her, the expression on his face that of genial, calm appraisal.

"Why yes," Tess said.

His hooded green eyes shined a smile on Tess as though he had all the time in the world, that it was just the two of them. But beneath the bonhomie, there was an undercurrent of danger. "And who might you be?" There was a soft, raspy tone to his voice, the likes of which Tess had never heard before.

"Hi there," she stammered as her heart seemed to pulse fearful exhilaration, "I'm Tess."

"You look like a Tess, kiddo."

The kitchen doors crashed opened as though ready to come off their hinges. Tony approached the man with hand extended. "Jake, great to see you."

They shook hands, and Tony faked a left jab toward Jake, who bobbed his head to the side and flashed a toothy grin. No doubt about it—this was a handsome man.

Tony leaned his head toward Tess, who was trying hard not to seem too interested. "You meet my right-hand girl?" Tony said. "Tess, this is an old friend from the neighborhood, Jake Langeham."

Tess offered a polite little smile. "We met, sorta," she said as something nascent and churning to take form was stirring inside her. Was this the *something* she had been looking for?

"Jake's gonna be staying in the extra staff bedroom for a few days," Tony said.

"Oh," Tess said as she stole a glance at Jake, who winked and nodded as if to say, "It'll be fine, kiddo." There was an exotic roughness about this man, so confident in his physical stature, in his place in the world, and he was rocking her world with so little effort other than being who he was—Jake Langeham.

"Let's catch up," Tony said to Jake with a slap on the back. He put his arm over Jake's shoulder and guided him to the other side of the bar, grinning big, both men laughing softly and talking quietly in that easy, comfortable manner when in the company of a longtime friend.

By midafternoon, a few customers had come into the dining area, which kept Tess busy enough that she wasn't standing across the bar from Jake and Tony with nothing to do. This lull period had never bothered her in the past; in fact, she looked forward to it, to catch her breath before the dinner crowd. But Jake had upset her equilibrium, and every time she returned to the bar, she tried her damnedest not to look at Jake but couldn't help stealing sideway glances over at him.

When Stacy returned to the tavern, she told Tess that the transmission on her car was shot and she had sold it to the mechanic for parts. "Good thing you got Teddy on board for our trip," Stacy said as her gaze drifted across the bar toward Tony and Jake in hushed conversation. "Who's the stud?"

"Jake Langeham."

"What a name," Stacy said. "He looks like a guy you wouldn't want to cross."

"He called me kiddo." Tess took a peek across the bar. Jake caught it, and out of the corner of his eye, he winked back at Tess.

"I think somebody's got an admirer," Stacy whispered.

"He's staying in the room next to ours."

"Whoa," Stacy said as she and Tess exchanged looks.

Tess was relieved at the arrival of the evening rush, and her mind shifted away from Jake Langeham. The dinner workload progressed as usual with her and Stacy waiting the tables efficiently, save one hiccup that Tess defused. A busboy had spilled a half-filled strawberry daiquiri on the lap of Mrs. Eleanor Phillips, a rich and widowed biddy, who screamed her displeasure, "Good God, boy, whatever have you done?"

Tess swooped in with a dry cloth and a bowl containing a water-based mixture she had learned about back in her country club days. "May I help?" Tess said as she dipped the end of the cloth in the bowl and showed it to Mrs. Phillips.

"What is it?"

"Club soda and water," Tess said as she eyed the dark red stain just above the right knee.

"All right, but if my slacks are ruined …" Mrs. Phillip stammered as her wrinkled face, which was normally a ghostly white, blushed light pink like a wilting, faded rose. She crossed her arms across her chest, puckered chin tucked into neck, sitting there like royalty awaiting one of her subjects to fix the problem.

Tess bent down on one knee and with her thumb and index finger lifted the gray cotton material, which was luxuriously soft, dabbing the damp end of the cloth on the stain, then back in the bowl, quickly and confidently applying the remedy. She then brushed the area with the dry end of the cloth until all that remained was a faintly wet gray spot, the stain miraculously gone.

"Well, I'll be," Mrs. Phillip said. She nodded at Tess—the queen excusing her subject.

Tony had observed all this from the safe distance of the bar. When Tess returned, he said, "I knew when you called about the job, you were what this joint needed, especially after some of the ding-dongs I've had working for me."

By ten o'clock, the girls were sitting at the bar counting their tips. "Not a bad night," Stacy said as she slapped a wad of bills on the edge of the bar before folding them over and stuffing them in the front pocket of her shorts.

"Notice anything different about tonight?" Tess said.

"Tony wasn't around."

"I bet our new dorm mate has something to do with it."

"Tony told me to close up," Teddy said as he wiped the bar down with a rag. "Only the second time." He gave the bar a final sweep and shrugged, then lifted an eyebrow toward Tess. "You girls want a ride into town?" he said as he shifted his gaze to Stacy and then back to Tess.

"Nah," Tess said as she glanced at Stacy, who remained noncommittal. "I could use a night off the bar scene."

"Does our new neighbor have something to do with it?" Teddy said.

Tess squished her face up as if she had never heard such a thing. "No, Teddy. Can't I stay in every now and then?"

"Sure thing," Teddy said.

The girls went into the kitchen to say good night to Papa Charlie, a loose-limbed, mostly legs and elbows, older black man with an engaging personality. Though never formally trained, Papa was a skilled and lightning-quick cook. He had worked in kitchens across the country for over thirty years and had an unlimited supply of stories about characters he had met.

"Gonna give them pub-crawling preppy boys something to look at tonight?" Papa said in a rumbly voice that seemed to have been primed by cigarettes and whiskey. He cocked his head, his large, dark eyes shining delight to his words.

When Tess told Papa they were staying in, he twirled his hand in the air with a regal flourish. "Let Papa make you a batch of my Mississippi down-home taters that be good to the last bite." He offered a pronounced nod and then went right to it. Lickety-split, he julienned four large potatoes into thin strips and slid the tubers in a deep fryer, which hissed and sizzled, filling the kitchen with the aroma of steamy-hot goodness.

While the girls waited, Papa told a story about working on the Delta Queen back in the fifties. His stories were short and sweet, blending drama and humor, and each one had a beginning, middle, and end. Papa Charlie never got past the fifth grade but was wise in ways of the world, which came across in his stories.

Papa Charlie generously seasoned the steaming, golden-brown potatoes with "my grand-pap's secret seasoning." He packed the finished product in a brown lunch bag and tucked it in a plastic bag along with a Styrofoam plate, napkins, and packets of ketchup. "There you go, ladies," Papa Charlie said as he handed the bag to Stacy and offered a crooked, left-handed salute off the corner of his eyebrow. "Not only a story about Cuban Henry, the riverboat gambler, but Papa's deee-lightful taters."

Up in their room, Stacy emptied the still steaming-hot fries on the Styrofoam plate. Tess then squeezed a couple of packets of ketchup on the side.

Their living quarters were small but more than adequate with a private bath, bedroom with two single beds, and a cozy living space with a worn but comfy sofa—on which they sat—rectangular nautical table that had seen better days, two plain armchairs, and a TV next to a stone fireplace, each of which they had never used. Along a wall was a double casement window with a view of the Atlantic Ocean.

"If these taste half as good as they smell," Stacy said as she dipped a fry into a pool of ketchup.

"Oh yeah," Tess said as both girls began scarfing down Papa Charlie's treat.

"Papa Charlie's Mississippi down-home taters *be* good to the last bite," Stacy said, lowering her voice a couple of octaves, imitating the cook as she wagged a fry at Tess before they both broke out laughing.

"I love his stories," Tess said. "Funny and deep at the same time." She looked at Stacy. "You know what I mean?"

"Yes," Stacy said. "Tonight, the ending, where the Cuban lost not only all his money to that hoodlum in a rigged poker game but his girlfriend too ..." Stacy squinted as if trying to remember. "What were Papa's exact words at the end?"

"'There are different kinds of wins and losses, and on that night, Cuban Henry won at life.'"

"Sometimes I think he's subtly preaching to us," Stacy said.

"Yeah," Tess said as she reached for a pack of cards on the table. "How about a game of gin rummy?"

"Why not," Stacy said. "Too early for bed."

They played cards for a couple of hours, talking and laughing about their summer in the Hamptons, including the new arrival. "Jake would make the perfect antihero," Stacy said as she discarded.

"Maybe he already is," Tess said as she drew a card, rearranged her hand, and discarded.

"Yeah," Stacy said, drawing a card, "glamour and danger all in one package."

She then discarded and laid her hand down. "Gin."

"What?" Tess said in a tone of surprise at not only Stacy's gin but also her comment on Jake.

"I think he likes you, Tess," Stacy said while counting her points. "So does Teddy boy. He's kinda cute in a chubby-cheeked sort of way." Stacy raised her brow, trying to get a reaction from Tess.

"He's a nice boy," Tess said.

"Yeah, but he's no Jake Langeham."

They burst out laughing. Tess leaned back, her head shaking, and said, "No, I believe the mold was broken when Mr. Langeham was born." She tilted her head toward the wall behind the sofa. "Kind of a scary excitement having *him* in the next room."

"Yeah, but kind of safe too." Stacy cocked her head toward the door at the pad of footsteps that stopped at their door. There was a knock. They looked at each other, each gaping with a cringe of horrified delight. Stacy got up and opened the door.

It was only Teddy, standing there glassy-eyed, a tumble of curls falling over his forehead, the dimpled cheeks flushed, and the long lashes flickering with roguish charm. He was holding a six-pack of beer and had a fat doobie secured behind his ear. "Thought you girls might like a cold one before turning in for the evening." He removed the joint from his ear. "Possibly a little marahooty aperitif before cocktails, ladies?" With hand gripping wrist, he offered the marijuana in his open palm, a cartoonish expression on his face—the bottom lip hung low in a *duh*, the eyebrow raised ala Groucho Marx, and the eyes rolling every which way.

"No, dope, funny boy," Stacy said. "I don't want to stink up our room."

"Fine," Teddy said as he put the joint back on his ear and held up the beer.

Stacy shrugged and looked back at Tess. "What'd you say, Tess?"

"Why not," Tess said.

Teddy took a seat in one of the armchairs, ripped three beers out of their plastic rings, and handed one to each of the girls. "Couple of guys at Moran's were asking about you two."

Tess started to say something but stopped at the creak of a door opening in the hallway. "Oh," she said as the door closed shut.

"You know," Teddy said as he tapped the pop top with two fingers before cracking it open, "he's nearly old enough to be your father."

"Please, Teddy," Stacy said, pausing to take a swallow of her beer, "stop trying to read our minds."

"Okay," Teddy said, leaning forward in his chair, an impish grin across his cherub face. "Tell me, ladies, what exactly do you think of Mr. Jake Langeham and what is he doing here at the Crock?"

The girls got up at eight and changed into their bathing suits. While Stacy wore a one-piece, Tess dressed in a high-waist bikini, which Stacy referred to as a "cop-out bikini." Tess had considered the skimpier bright red version in a department store back home when a sales lady came by and told her that she would look *fabulous* in it. "It takes a certain body type and also a certain attitude to feel comfortable in," the woman told Tess. "You have the body, but your expression tells me that maybe this," she said, lifting up a high-waist bikini, "would make you feel more comfortable." So, Tess took the woman's advice and played it safe, settling for middle ground in her style of bathing suit. "But next time," she had told herself. "Next time."

After a night away from the hubbub of the bar scene and a good night's sleep, Tess felt refreshed and rested. With beach carryalls in hand, she and Stacy walked the short distance to Crockford Beach. It was low tide, and they spread a blanket behind and off to the side of the lifeguard stand.

Crockford Beach was a long stretch of fine white sand with a smattering of umbrellas, under which were mostly older people—Tess spotted a couple she had waited on last night, reading in beach chairs at the water's edge. The smell of surf, suntan lotion, and hamburgers grilling at the snack bar located at the pavilion in front of the sand dunes wafted through the air. The sky was blue and the temperature warm but the humidity low for a change—a perfect beach day.

Tess sat down on the blanket, shielding her eyes, elbow resting on raised knee as she scanned the beach. About twenty yards down, a man stood at the edge of the water. He was of medium height, but his body was lean and muscular as though sculpted. He seemed at ease, his head tilted ever so slightly to the side in an insouciant manner.

Tess looked over at Stacy, who was stretched out on her stomach, opening a paperback. "I see *him*, Stacy."

"Let me guess," Stacy said as she rolled over and sat up. "He's built like some Greek god."

"Adonis to be exact," Tess said, her eyes on Jake Langeham as he bolted into the water and dove into a wave. He came up and swam out past the break, his strokes strong like a lifeguard's.

"He brings a new meaning to interesting in a dark sort of way," Stacy said as both girls watched Jake swim parallel to the shoreline.

Tess put on a pair of tortoise-shelled sunglasses, watching Jake come out of the water and sit on a short white towel facing the ocean. Through the shielded lens, the glare of the sun neutralized, she saw Jake in a different light, in a different world where she could let her imagination go, not restrained by inhibition and upbringing. Tess was looking at Jake through her own private looking glass. She thought of the words to the Paul Simon song "Kodachrome": "Everything looks worse in black and white."

"What sort of ancestry do you think Langeham is?" Tess said.

"Not Italian," Stacy said, eyeballing Jake from the corner of her eye. "What would you say if he asked you out?"

"What would you say?" Tess said.

"I'm not his type—too tall, for one thing." Stacy tilted her head toward Tess, a neat little smile tucked in the corner of her mouth. "He'd go for a good-looking, golden-skin brunette about five foot six, great figure, and not too chatty." She raised her eyebrows in an inquisitive manner. "Know anyone who fits the bill?"

Tess kept her focus on Jake as he lay down on his back, knees raised. If he did ask her out, where would they go and what would they talk about? He didn't seem the type to fit into the bars they hung out at in town—too young a crowd and probably not his style. Did she even know what his style was? Brooklyn cool? Older-guy cool? The image of her and Jake floated into her mind unannounced. They were sharing a blanket on a deserted island beach, little conversation, both reeking of spongy, sweaty sex after an exhaustive, satisfying night in a palm-leafed hut.

She wasn't sure what was causing these wild fantasies and wondered if when she smuggled the job application flyers in the student union, it didn't trigger this internal metamorphosis, which very possibly may have been a long time coming.

In high school, Tess had been heavy and a bit of a loner. She didn't have her first date until senior year of high school, and the boy was a nerdy type who was too shy to kiss her good night. But by the end of freshman year at Maryland, she had lost weight, partially because the dining hall food was not very good, and without a car that first year, she was constantly walking from one end of the large campus to get to her classes, the dining halls, and her dorm. And even more so, the uncertainty of living on her own had knocked Tess out of her comfort zone, causing a little motor to run constantly inside her—she could almost feel the weight shedding itself like a molting winter coat.

By sophomore year, guys were taking notice: glances of admiration in class, phone calls from boys she barely knew asking her out. It thrilled her and scared her. She met Buddy in Sociology 101 when he asked to borrow a pen. His good looks were illuminated by his boyish shyness, and it drew her to him. Soon they were dating, and Tess had her first boyfriend and only lover. Thinking of Buddy brought a disquieting stir in her bones before dismissing them, since she hadn't done anything in regard to Jake but have a few wild fantasies. Guys had them all the time, so why couldn't she fantasize about an intriguing older guy?

Tony would not approve of Tess and Jake together, and Tess figured Jake knew that, and if her fantasy were true, he would ask her out when the boss wasn't around. And if he did ask, it came over her that she would have a hard time saying no. She wanted to know what it would be like to be with him, to have him pay attention to her, talk to her, tell her his secrets. Boyfriend or not, saying no did not seem an option, Tess told herself as she watched Jake extend his legs out and clasp his fingers behind his neck. Droplets of water glistened on his chest and stomach. Adonis in repose.

Tess had taken a Greek mythology course last semester as an elective and learned that Adonis was the god of beauty and desire. This was probably a crazy fantasy on her part—the sun slipping behind a billowy pure-white cloud broke her train of thought momentarily, darkening her perspective through the looking glass—but even so, a little voice told her to be careful, very careful, for she was in over her head with Jake Langeham.

By one that afternoon, the tavern was packed with local business types and women casually but expensively dressed in silk and cashmere and with that air of Southampton entitlement. At the waitress station, the girls converged to give their drink orders to the daytime bartender, Johnny. He was a retired New York City firefighter, with a trace of a brogue from the old country and a perpetual smile on his ruddy-cheeked face, which was in perfect contrast to his thinning white hair. As Johnny prepared the drink orders, Stacy said to Tess, "I'd rather be dead broke and homeless than carry on like those old biddies." She leaned her head over her shoulder in the direction of a table of six women ranging in age from fifty to eighty, all bejeweled in gold and silver on their wrists and necks, like tribal decorations signifying their status. To Tess, they were people who had gotten their way all their lives, wielding power with money and a long lineage of upper-class ancestors.

Johnny put an order of margaritas in front of Stacy. "Here you go, Stacy me girl." He grinned and said, "What's the occasion?"

"The *ladies* are flying to Cabo, and as Mrs. Van Houghton said, 'Oh, my darlings,'" Stacy said with a dead-on haughty accent, "'we must, yes we must, have margaritas.'"

Tess and Johnny broke out in a guffaw of laughter. Stacy stacked the drinks on a tray and whisked herself off. Tess gave Johnny her order. He poured gin and dry vermouth into a metal shaker filled with ice and shook the shaker over his shoulder, then began pouring the contents into martini glasses. "I met the new boarder," he said out of the side of his mouth, as though delivering big news.

Tess nodded silently.

Johnny speared three olives with toothpicks to finish off the martinis. "Charming lad, that Jake." Johnny nodded as if to confirm his words. "He told me he's half-Irish. Only one of Tony pals that isn't Italian." Johnny said this as an observation, with no hint of malice.

After the lunch rush had waned, the bar empty, except Tess and Stacy sitting at the corner next to the waitress station, Johnny had asked Tess to watch the bar for a moment while he used the pay phone to place a bet with his bookie. "These double shifts getting to you?" Stacy asked Tess.

Tess checked the dining area where her last table was drinking coffee. "It's okay. What about you?"

"Can't beat the money," Stacy said. "I guess we have the Ellington sisters to thank."

They were two local girls, one just finished high school, the other, two years in college. Both had constantly arrived late to work, which infuriated Tony, who finally asked Tess and Stacy if they could work double shifts for the remainder of their employment. When they agreed, he fired the sisters. Tony had told Tess that those born with a silver spoon in the mouth were terrible employees. "You know, Tess, in my fourteen months here, not one of them snooty ding-dong girls has lasted."

By five, the bar was nearly full, including a cluster of local college-age boys, in shorts and polo shirts, situated near the waitress station. Like their elders, they flaunted that air of superiority. The leader of the pack was a dark-haired fellow—well over six feet, lean athletic build— who had rowed crew for Harvard.

On more than one occasion, he had tried to talk up Tess, who always answered politely and quickly scurried away.

The dining area was still slow, so Tess told Stacy she would handle the dining room for the next hour. So, Stacy went up to their room to relax.

Soon after, the Harvard boy came over and sat on the stool next to the waitress station. "How are you? Tess, isn't it? Some of us are driving out to Montauk Point later this evening to party on the beach."

Tess said nothing, her expression blank.

"Would you like to come with me?" He smiled, revealing a row of strong teeth, white as snow. "I'm driving a 450 SL convertible, top down." He raised his eyebrows as though demanding an answer.

As Tess turned to walk away, he put his long arm, corded with muscle, up against her waist.

"Excuse me," Tess said.

The boy stood and faced Tess, blocking her exit. "What do you say?"

Tess tried to move around him, but he stepped over, blocking her path.

An authoritative voice came from across the bar, a confident alpha male voice, dripping with street swagger. "Leave her be."

Tess looked over and saw Jake sitting at the bar. He was wearing a maroon, tight-knit, short-sleeve shirt. He looked like a well-conditioned prize fighter. An expectant hush fell over the bar.

Harvard looked at Jake, who had honed his eyes into two narrow slits, his jaw clenched, and his hands folded on the bar as though prepared to pray. A dazed, out-of-his-league look came over the boy, who a moment ago was so cocky and sure of himself. His mouth opened hesitantly, and Jake cocked his head off to the side, his expression stone cold.

The boy's friends were standing there, their bottom lips hanging out in an *oh shit* expression.

"Walk away," Jake said evenly. "Walk away now." Jake flashed a hard look at the friends and then back at Harvard, who backed up and then turned and walked away, his friends in tow.

Johnny, who was behind the bar, gave Jake the thumbs-up and said in a low voice, "Score one for the Irish boy from the city."

Jake let out a little laugh, as if he hadn't a care in the world. He got up and walked around the bar, every eye on him—the champ exiting the ring—and took the seat that Harvard had been sitting in. He looked at Tess standing next to him, his eyes now soft and gentle. All the tension had left his face, which moments ago had a controlled fierceness. He placed his hand on Tess's shoulder. "You okay, kiddo?"

"I am now. Thanks, Jake."

Johnny came over to Jake. "What are you drinking?"

"Chivas, straight up," Jake said as he gave Tess's shoulder a little squeeze and two taps before removing his hand.

Tess wanted to gush all over Jake, wanted to let this dizzying moment last. To tell him how very cool he'd been just then and that he had even scared her a little bit. But something she couldn't put a name to told her to be careful here. That Jake Langeham, for all his chivalry, had a side to him that functioned with sniper efficiency.

Johnny placed Jake's drink in front of him. "On the house, Jake Langeham."

Jake nodded a thank-you. He then turned to Tess and tapped the seat next to him. "Come sit with me for a bit, kiddo."

Tess checked the dining area, which was still quiet, and did as the gentleman from Brooklyn requested.

By the time Stacy returned to the tavern, things were beginning to pick up in the dining room, with couples anywhere from thirty-five up to Mr. and Mrs. Roberts, who were well into their eighties.

The Roberts arrived every Friday promptly at six, and each had one Old Fashioned, followed by the soup of the day and a glass of wine with dinner. They never had dessert and were always gone by seven fifteen. They talked to each other in low murmurs as though speaking a secret language. They didn't act snobby but were not overly friendly either. They always said good evening to their server when first approached and good evening at departure. They were both from old money, according to Teddy. Mr. Roberts had made another fortune on Wall Street and still worked five days a week, taking the train into the city.

The Roberts were halfway through their cocktail, signaling Tess that it was time to take their appetizer order, which she already knew would be Manhattan clam chowder. Everything about them indicated an orderly air of no nonsense, from his dark sports coat, white shirt, and bow tie to her neatly pressed slacks and short-sleeve blouse with starched collar. Neither wore a lot of trinkets, as their contemporaries did; instead, each wore a watch and wedding band, and that was it. They were no muss, no fuss, but with it came a confident, righteous air. Tess, in a way, admired them for their differences, not going along with the money crowd. She approached and asked if they were ready to order an appetizer.

"Yes," Mr. Roberts said, stringing the word out, which was unusual. "We'd like …" He stopped in midsentence and looked around the room as though to see if anyone was listening. "I hear there was a bit of a confrontation earlier."

"Oh," Tess said as she tried to collect herself. "It wasn't anything really."

Mrs. Robert put her hand on Tess's wrist. "Now, dear, we don't get much excitement around here. Do tell."

"A local boy and a friend of Tony had some words." Tess straightened as if that was all there was to it. "Are you getting the clam chowder?"

"Yes, we are," Mr. Roberts said. "The Browton boy bullied our grandson all through prep school."

Tess saw a trace of sorrow in the old man's expression that was suddenly soft and vulnerable.

"I don't know his name—tall, dark hair, recently graduated from Harvard?"

"That's him," Mrs. Roberts said.

"He was trying to get me to go out with him, and when he didn't get his way, he blocked my path. Tony's friend intervened."

"He sounds heroic," Mrs. Roberts piped in.

"Yes, he is," Tess said as she saw that both were hungry for justice. "He told Browton to walk away from me."

"That is all he said?" Mr. Roberts said.

"Yes, sir, that's it," Tess replied.

By ten o'clock that evening, the dining room was empty, and only one customer remained at the bar finishing his drink. Tess and Stacy were sitting at the end of the bar while Teddy was closing out the cash register. "Hey, Stacy, did you hear about Sir Galahad rescuing Tess earlier?"

"What?" Stacy said, looking at Teddy and then Tess. "What's this about?"

Tess filled Stacy in on the confrontation and then mentioned her conversation with Jake afterward. "He asked me to sit with him."

"Yeah?" Stacy said.

"Next thing I know, he's telling me about growing up in Brooklyn in the late forties: stealing cars in Manhattan, running numbers, turf wars with local gangs—'We were the real-life Sharks and Jets.'"

"I wish he had knocked the snot out of that punk Harvard kid," Stacy said.

Teddy came over to the girls. "Tony told me his hands are registered with the authorities as lethal weapons." He removed a rag from his shoulder and began to wipe down the bar. "Says he was a Golden Gloves boxing champ."

"Seems …" Stacy said, "that Sir Galahad has many sides to him."

Teddy stowed his rag under the bar. "Seems …" he said, mimicking Stacy with a marveling nod for good measure, "I'm off tomorrow and feel like a sailor on liberty." Teddy smiled big. "I'm going to Moran's shortly." He looked at Tess, an inquiring eyebrow raised.

Tess squinted. *Maybe.*

"Come on, Tess," Stacy said with a lift in her voice. "We need to celebrate the rescue of the fair maiden from Bethesda, Maryland, by the dark knight from Flatbush."

"Jake asked me if I was going anywhere tonight."

"What!" Stacy shrieked.

"I told him we might be going to Moran's."

"Oh, we are definitely going—even if I have to drag you," Stacy said.

Moran's was a loud, raucous, hell-of-a-good-time joint. It had a circular bar in the center of the space, with booths along walls on two sides and sturdy wooden tables here and there. College pennants and sports memorabilia hung everywhere, and on a back wall was a rural landscape mural from another time and place: thatched cottages, a furrowed field with a man and woman, both barefoot, digging and loading potatoes into a basket, a little white dog nearby, watching them.

It was in odd juxtaposition to the trendy group of customers in their twenties.

At the bar, Teddy asked a couple if they would move their seat down to make room for three to stand at the corner of the bar. "No," the guy said and then turned his attention back to his date. But Teddy just kept an easy grin on his face and said to the girl, "You don't mind, do you?" She got off her stool and raised her chin for her date to do as requested. He slid the chairs down, and the threesome bellied up to the bar.

Teddy's real name was William, but his older sister called him Teddy because, as he told Tess the first time the three went out on the town, "She said I reminded her of a teddy bear." He had shrugged and said, "If the shoe fits, wear it." And with a baby face and that incorrigible tumble of wavy brown hair and eyes that shined a warm welcome like full moons, he was the type of guy that people liked at first sight.

Tess thought of him more like a brother, but she had sensed from the get-go that Teddy was sweet on her: lingering looks of admiration here and there, stop-everything attentiveness when she spoke, offering his smile when catching her eye.

But she already had a boyfriend, though far away and disappearing from her radar, and now Jake had upset her equilibrium with his oblique, cool-guy interest in her. Would he show? She wondered, glancing at the front door as a raucous group of college-aged boys entered dressed in T-shirts and flip-flops.

The jukebox was blaring out oldies over the din, the beer flowing, and everyone was having a grand old time. Teddy stood between the two girls and ordered three drafts. When their beers arrived, Stacy lifted her mug and said in a raised voice, "A toast to Sir Jake from Brooklyn and all the other brave men who roam this land far and wide and save fair damsels in distress."

Teddy broke up into hooting laughter. At first, Tess tried to fight it, but she soon began laughing. All the while, she kept her eyes on the lookout for the arrival of Jake. She imagined what it would be like when he walked in. Would the music stop and everyone turn and look at this cool, dark character from another world? Or would he not show?

Stacy looked around the bar with a daredevil gleam in her eyes. "I think we need to take a survey of the guys in this bar and see how they would have handled the situation."

Part of Tess wanted to stop Stacy, which she knew wouldn't happen anyway, and another part said, *What the heck? Let's have some fun.*

Stacy waved the bartender over, who was a big-shouldered longshoreman sort of guy. "Girl at your bar getting hassled by member of Harvard crew who won't leave her alone. Puts hands on girl." Stacy leaned toward the bartender, a what-would-you-do expression on her face.

He made a fist with his big-knuckled hand. "I'd knock him out just for you."

"Yeah!" Stacy shouted. "Score one for chivalry."

A group of guys had drifted over, curious about what this tall young woman was all about.

"You there, cutie," Stacy said, pointing to a tanned, shaggy-haired blond guy who looked like a lifeguard. "What about you?"

A big smile split his face. "I'd take him for a long swim, one way."

"Now we're talking," Stacy said as she raised her mug toward Blondie, who clinked her glass with his.

And so the evening began, with Stacy holding court, Teddy adding a bon mot every now and then, and Tess listening and laughing and checking the front door. As the evening progressed, and just as Tess had begun to lose hope that Jake would show, she turned as she felt a hand squeeze her shoulder.

"Hello, kiddo."

"Jake," Tess said as she felt a rush of desire and fear.

Jake was wearing a New York Yankees ball cap and was dressed in khaki Bermuda shorts, a plain gray T-shirt, and sneakers with no socks. He didn't seem anywhere near as out of place as Tess had thought—older, yes, but so at ease.

Tess started to introduce Teddy and Stacy, but Jake said, "Stacy and Teddy, right?" Jake bowed his head slightly toward Stacy, who for once had nothing to say as she smiled big at Jake, who then offered his hand to Teddy. "So, what are we drinking, Teddy?"

Jake ordered another round of beers, and Teddy asked about a guy from Brooklyn wearing a Yankees cap.

"Only kid in my neighborhood who rooted for the Yankees." Jake shrugged and said, "I liked winners. Still do." A small smile seemed to come to his eyes. "Got in more than a few fights over that little matter."

A momentary lull came over the foursome as Jake stood there, with beer in hand, his elbow tucked to his waist, his gaze keen, taking the moment in. The other three looked at Jake with expectation, a look that said *the ball is in your court.*

Jake said, "This looks like a joint in my old neighborhood but with a different set of characters." He lifted his chin in the general direction of the mural of old Ireland. "My great-grandparents on my mother's side came over during the great famine. Stories about that period were passed down through the generations." Jake studied the mural, and for just a moment, Tess saw a wince of empathy for his ancestral people, before it vanished, and with it, a noncommittal grin emerged. "Tough times, they were, that made tough people." After a momentary pause, he added, "That is, if they lived."

Tess noticed that Stacy was looking at Jake as if he were some rare, interesting new species where silent observance was required, and it came over Tess that she felt the same way and then some.

Teddy asked if he had visited Ireland. "No," he said in tone that indicated he was not interested. Jake mentioned that he had been all over the European continent. "Still got a lot of the old-world values over there," he said.

"Like an eye for an eye," Stacy said.

"Sure," Jake said as he looked over at the Irish mural.

"I bet you've been all around the world, Jake," Teddy said.

"Seen some places," Jake said. "Hong Kong, Malaysia, Singapore, all about the Orient ..." A remembering look came over Jake as if he were recollecting an old escapade.

Jake never got specific about himself and his life, everything on the periphery, and all the while he shot a subtle glance every now and then in Tess's direction—a friendly look but also an alluring look, a *going my way, kiddo* look—that suggested an adjustable moral compass. And with the looks came a tap on the wrist or shoulder, leaning into her to emphasize a point. Little touches here and there that sent seismic shock waves through Tess.

Tess felt such a tug of attraction to this complex man of mystery that she thought of the sailors in the *Odyssey*, putting wax in their ears to prevent hearing the Sirens' song. But she had no figurative wax, and even if she did, she was too wrapped in the moment. As were Stacy and Teddy, who were listening to every word from Jake as though he were the Pied Piper with a magnetic vibe. Also, more than a few girls and some guys were stealing a peek at this stud in the Yankees ball cap, his watchful guard temporarily down, in a sea of sudsy youth.

Jake had done his homework on his companions for the evening. He asked Teddy about NYU law school and commented that his cousin had graduated from there as an undergrad. He told them that he was offered a partial scholarship to Maryland to play football. "But I broke my leg that summer, and they went back on their word." He lifted his shoulders with palms up at chest level. "No biggie," he said as he made a face, and it seemed a curtain had been pulled back, and for an instant there was a glimmer of doubt—it might have been different.

Eventually, Jake suggested they take a seat in a booth, and next thing Tess knew, she was sitting next to Jake, arms and legs touching, across from Stacy and Teddy. Tess was feeling pleasantly high from the beers, and she knew that Stacy and Teddy were also. Jake, she could not tell. He had that same actor-on-cue presence that Tony had but with a much more appealing persona.

"I hear you went to prep school, Teddy," Jake said. "What was that like?" His voice was sincere, as though he and Teddy were alone, old pals sharing a drink.

Teddy mentioned good academics and the history of the place. "Two presidents have graduated from there."

"Come on, Teddy," Stacy said as she leaned her shoulder into his. "Jake wants to hear about some brash preppy adventure." Stacy raised her brow and leaned her head across the table. "Am I right, Jake?"

Jake wagged a finger at Stacy. "You're on to me."

"Okay," Teddy said as he took a long swallow of his beer, finishing it. He wiped his mouth with the back of his hand and then proceeded to tell a story about stealing a pig from a nearby farm, somehow getting it into the back of his car, and in the middle of the night breaking into the school and leaving it in the dean of students' office over a weekend.

"Monday morning," Teddy said with a remembering shake of the head, "you could smell the stench as soon as you entered the school. Never did discover who was responsible."

Jake laughed heartily with hands on chest. "Teddy—who knew? Such an innocent face."

Everyone was now in grand spirits as another pitcher of beer arrived, and Stacy poured beers all around. It seemed Jake fit right in with these three young people like an old, comfortable glove.

Tess then mentioned sharing a dorm room freshman year with Stacy. "And soon I discovered she was wrapped a little differently." Tess told of Stacy taking a goose on a leash to their first keg party.

"It was going fine and dandy," Stacy added, "until it laid a big green turd on a table." She shrugged and said, "It was like a Dr. Seuss story gone haywire."

"You're killing me." Jake laughed as he leaned back, his hands raised as if surrendering.

Teddy asked Jake what it was like growing up in Brooklyn as a kid.

"Freedom," Jake said. "We were as wild as the wind." He looked off for a moment and then reached under the table for Tess's hand and took it in his. "I got nothing but good memories of those days." The finality in his tone made it was clear that he had no more to say on the matter. And it came over Tess that he had revealed much more about his youthful indiscretions to her after running Harvard boy from the bar.

Jake squeezed Tess's hand, and she squeezed back, barely able to contain a growing clamor of desire. His hand was strong but gentle, and there was a soothing warmth to it.

The overhead lights flickered off and on, signaling last call, and Teddy ordered a round of schnapps. After Teddy paid—he insisted, and Jake did not argue—they got up and departed Moran's. At the front door, Jake offered his hand toward the sidewalk and said, "Ladies first." Jake walked alongside Teddy, with Tess and Stacy in front. When they got back to the Crockford Inn, Tess wasn't sure what Jake was going to do. Would he ask her to take a walk on the beach? Come to his room? She had the most overpowering sense that she could not say no to him. She was under his spell. Sir Jake, the Brooklyn lancer, the dark knight with the roguish charm and sex appeal.

In the hallway to their rooms, Teddy said good night and weaved his way to his door, fumbled with his key and finally opened the door and went in.

Jake stood outside Tess and Stacy's door, his green eyes, like emerald gems, smiling at Tess. He slid a look at Stacy that suggested a private moment.

Stacy stood her ground for a second and then looked at Tess, who nodded okay.

Stacy entered the room, leaving the door ajar.

"I enjoy your company, kiddo." Jake reached for Tess's hands and held them up to his chest. He leaned forward and kissed her, bringing her into him, his arms around her waist.

Jake stepped back from Tess, still holding her hands. He looked at her, and in his gaze, Tess saw conflict. Was he worried about Tony finding out, or was it more likely that his moral compass leaned toward righteousness?

Tess wanted to tilt it the other way. She wanted him to guide her to his room and let come what may.

Jake released Tess's hands, bowed his head, and said, "Good night, kiddo."

The beeping alarm on the clock radio went off at its usual time of eight. Tess rolled over and turned it off.

"What a night," Stacy said as she sat on the edge of the bed and stretched her arms over her head, yawning big. "Okay, Tess, what happened last night?" When Tess had come in, she told Stacy they would talk in the morning.

Tess told Stacy about holding hands under the table at Moran's and the kiss in the hallway. "If he had asked me to his room, I would have gone, Stacy. I would have done it."

"Tess," Stacy said in a tone that Tess had never heard before from her friend, "be careful with him. Just, please, be careful."

They looked at each other for a moment before Stacy said, "Let's take a dip in the ocean." She stood, dressed in her gray cotton nightgown, the sleeves of which she had cut off at the shoulders like a muscle shirt.

When Tess had asked why she cut the sleeves, Stacy had replied, "In case some rapscallion breaks into our room and wants to have his way with us." She flexed her bicep, showing off an impressive rock of muscle. "He'll know that the iron maiden will have none of it." Oh, how Tess had laughed at that answer. Stacy was her one-of-a-kind friend.

It was already warm at Crockford Beach; today would be a scorcher. Stacy dropped her carryall and ran hell-bent into the ocean, dove right into a wave, and came up screaming and waving for Tess to join her.

"Okay," Tess said, "give me a minute." She was thinking about Stacy's warning about Jake and knew she was right, but she also realized she was in the midst of a transformation. What it encompassed and where it would lead, she did not know. But there was something inside her wanting to break loose, consequences be damned.

At the water's edge, Tess waited for a wave to break and then walked out to her waist and dunked herself. Immediately, she felt refreshed, as though the toxins from last night had been cleansed from her body.

The girls swam along the shoreline for a few hundred yards and then back before returning to their blanket. They shielded their eyes, scanning the beach. There he was, down a ways, standing along the water's edge, squinting out to the ocean as though searching for something.

"He's seems really deep in thought," Stacy said. "Gotta wonder what he's doing at the Crock." Stacy looked at Tess, who kept her gaze on Jake.

Jake Langeham ran into the ocean, churning through the low water with the power and agility of a halfback breaking through the line. He dove into a wave and swam out past the break. "Strong swimmer," Stacy said as they both sat with hands behind their backs, legs extended, watching his every move.

A huge wave rolled toward Jake, and he swam toward the shore, catching the wave just as it crested. He bodysurfed, only his head visible, as he rode the monster up on the beach.

The girls exchanged *wow* looks. Tess wanted to draw his attention but wasn't sure where she stood with him. She didn't want to walk up to him and hear, "Last night was a mistake, kiddo," and then have to sheepishly walk back to her blanket and Stacy's silent scrutiny. But Tess didn't want him leaving without seeing her. She kept her gaze on him as he dried himself off and placed the towel around his neck. Jake turned to walk back to the inn. Tess was screaming in her head, *Look over here! Look over here!*

Jake stopped. His brow furrowed, and his eyes narrowed as he scanned the beach, stopping when he spotted the girls.

"Lookie, lookie," Stacy said under her breath as Jake approached.

Tess noticed the rippled row of muscle across his stomach, the skin dark gold, and the stride sure and confident, as though he owned the beach and everything in sight.

He came to halt in front of the girls, his eyes on Tess. "How you doing, kiddo?"

"Hi there" was all Tess could muster.

Jake turned his gaze on Stacy. "Mind if I steal her," he said, lifting his chin toward Tess, "for a walk down the beach?"

Without hesitation, Tess extended her hand to Jake, who helped her up.

Tess and Jake walked along the water's edge, their heels and toes leaving temporary footprints in the moist sand before the surf washed them away. Jake remained silent and did not take her hand in hers. Tess wondered if he did not like public displays, even something as innocuous as holding hands, or if he felt funny about the age difference.

Around a bend, they came to a deserted section of beach. Jake stopped and took Tess's hand in his. "Kiddo," he said, "you are one fine-looking woman." Tess leaned into Jake, and he brought her in close, his arms around her waist. He raised his mouth, his tongue finding hers with a hunger that she reciprocated.

The whining shifting of car gears broke the moment. Jake released his embrace, a quiver of tension in the eyes, the jaw clenched tight, his body seeming to hum with alertness. It was a beach patrol jeep rumbling its way down the beach. Driving it was Blondie the lifeguard from last night at Moran's, who Stacy had traded barbs with. As he passed, he offered a raised hand to Tess—sorry.

When they went back to where Stacy was, Jake raised his hand to say so long and then turned and walked off, a look here, a look there, as though making sure he wasn't being followed.

"Well?" Stacy said.

Tess watched Jake until he disappeared behind a dune and then filled Stacy in, including the walk back in silence.

"Not a word?" Stacy said.

"Like I wasn't there," Tess said.

"He has the look of a guy on the run," Stacy said. She looked at Tess, her apprehensive gaze smudged with curiosity. "You do realize how hopeless it is with him, don't you?"

They exchanged looks for a moment, Tess not wanting to face the reality of the situation.

"Last thing on this subject," Stacy said. "I will be there for you, Tess."

After lounging on their blanket for a while in preparation for another double shift, Tess and Stacy walked over to a little diner not far from the Crockford. They sat in a booth along a back wall and were waited on a by a waitress in her early thirties. Her name was Beverly, and they knew her casually from the bars, where she hung out with a group that worked in the local hotels and restaurants. They were an older, somewhat jaded crowd who could not seem to take the leap into adulthood, menial work by day in support of partying by night.

Beverly looked as though at one time she was a beauty, and though still attractive, the nightlife had taken its toll on her: creases projecting from the corners of her mouth and eyes, and a weariness about her, as if this life she had loved in her early twenties was conspiring against her. The girls exchanged hellos before Beverly commented, "Saw you two last night at Moran's." There was a matter-of-fact tone in her voice, a voice that said there was more to come.

"Oh, we didn't see you," Tess said. She looked at Stacy for confirmation, but Stacy stayed silent, her patient eyes on Beverly.

"That older guy you girls were with was one fine-looking stud duck."

Beverly leaned forward with both hands on the table, her bountiful breasts nearly spilling out of her low-cut blouse, her eyes glinting with sexual mischief. "Now what can I get you, girls?"

After Beverly took their order and left, Stacy gave Tess a knowing lift of her brow and said, "Well, that clinches it."

Tess looked at Stacy. *Go on. Get it all out.*

"Old Bev there is exhibit A, Professor, as to why this job will only be for the summer." Stacy raised a finger with an aha look of discovery.

"It is the summer of Tess and Stacy—a stepping-stone to bigger and better things."

After a shower, Tess and Stacy reported to work at eleven, a half hour before opening. They found Tony behind the bar, restocking the liquor supply. "Morning," Tony said in an edgy voice as he ripped open a carton of beer. His restless congeniality had been replaced by an air of beleaguered gruffness.

The kitchen doors swung open, and Papa Charlie emerged in his white kitchen jacket. "Hey, boss ..." Papa stopped talking when he saw the girls at the waitress station putting on their aprons. But even in those two words, *Hey, boss,* Tess noted a higher decibel level, as though something big was about to come down.

Tony motioned for Papa Charlie to head back into the kitchen. He then swung open the bar-top flapper door and hurried past the girls into the kitchen.

"I think something is up, and we both know who it's about," Stacy said.

It had been a busy double shift, with barely a lull between lunch and dinner. Around eight thirty, Jake had come into the bar, squinting a smile at Tess, but he seemed distracted, a look here, a look there. Tony poured him a Chivas straight up and nodded at Jake, who did the same.

Usually when Tony tended bar, he was talking with one and all—his broad laughs filling the space, mixing drinks with high energy—but not tonight. He was almost robotic.

At closing time, Stacy had volunteered to help Papa Charlie with a backlog of dirty dishes, and Tony had suddenly disappeared. Jake sat alone at the bar, his sharp gaze on constant surveillance, as if waiting for something to happen. Tess wanted to go over and sit with him. To have him tell her it would be all right, not to worry. She wanted him to hold her hand in his, to cast his spell over her. But there was an all-consuming watchfulness about him. She would wait and see.

When the pay phone rang, Jake looked over with an inquiring slant of the brow. The kitchen door burst open, and Papa Charlie answered. "Hey, Mr. Jake, phone call." There was an eager note in Papa's voice that announced that the something big was now coming down.

Jake answered, listened silently, and returned to his seat. He turned his attention to Tess. "Kiddo," he said, tapping the stool next to him.

Tess came over and sat. "Yes, Jake."

"I need a favor." He leaned his head toward her and whispered, "I gotta get on down the road." The flash of headlights drew Jake's attention to the front window for an instant before he said, "Can you spare a hundred?"

Tess felt an odd rippling in her stomach. She looked at Jake, and in his eyes, for the first time, she saw impatience and with it the wild, dangerous look of a caged animal. Tess reached into her tip apron and came up with four twenties, a ten, and ten singles. She stacked most of her night's earnings on the bar in a neat pile. "Hundred on the nose, Jake," she said, staring at the money.

Jake scooped up the bills, folded them, and secured them in his shirt pocket. "What if … kiddo." He was reassessing the situation when the heavy bang of car doors shutting registered like a warning shot. "Gotta go, Tess," Jake said in a detached voice, the voice of a man with nothing to lose. He tapped her on the shoulder and smiled and winked conspiratorially, and then he was gone like a ghost into the night, slipping through the swinging doors to the kitchen. Tess felt abandoned. She had been left in Jake's wake, probably not the first, probably not the last.

The forceful thud of the front door opening caused Tess to jump in her seat. She turned to see three men dressed in dark blue suits, thin black ties, and starched white shirts walking toward her. They had close-cropped haircuts with no sideburns and a superior I'm-in-charge demeanor.

The oldest of the three pointed to the kitchen door. "Delaney, check it out." The head guy then scanned the dining area, which was empty save one couple enjoying a late-night brandy. He motioned to the other agent. "Check out the rest of the place." He then directed his attention to Tess sitting all by her lonesome at the bar. "Do you know Jake Langeham?" He removed his fedora hat, which brought to mind Dick Tracy, and put it on the bar right where Jake had been no more than a minute ago.

She felt torn between loyalty to Jake—even though he had just left with no explanation and scammed her for money—and her upbringing of always doing the right thing. "Who wants to know?" Tess had no idea where her reply came from, but there it was.

The man straightened, reached inside his coat jacket, and flipped open his wallet. She saw the bold blue letters FBI, with his mug shot and below it a name, Inspector John O'Connor.

"Young lady." He leaned toward Tess, who caught a whiff of Old Spice and mouthwash. "It's a federal crime to harbor a fugitive."

Tess looked into the mirror behind the bar and thought how absurd the image of this hulking forty-year-old man in his government-issue suit trying to intimidate her was. She absentmindedly put her hand in her now nearly empty apron pocket and said, "I saw him earlier but don't know where he is now."

The agent who had been searching the dining area and bathrooms returned and stood on her other side. "Jake Langeham is wanted for check fraud and money laundering." There was an annoying nasal quality to his voice.

"Look," Tess said, "I just work here."

A loud, aggrieved voice blared from the kitchen. "Take your hands off me."

The kitchen door swung open, and Stacy stormed out, followed by Agent Delaney, who appeared to be no more than twenty-five.

"Inspector, I found her in a storage room." The young agent pointed his chin in Tess's direction. "Take a seat with your sidekick."

Stacy wheeled around and looked eye level at him. "Look, *buster*, we haven't done a damn thing other than wait tables and serve drinks."

The young agent made a gesture for Stacy to sit. She drew her chin in and stared back at him. He repeated the motion, and Stacy muttered, "Hmmph" before taking a seat next to Tess.

The inspector went behind the bar and faced Tess and Stacy, straightening the perfectly straight knot in his tie. "Where is Jake Langeham?"

Stacy shrugged and said, "Beats me."

His eyes shifted subtly to Tess, who felt like she was in some low-budget gangster movie. She didn't know whether to burst out laughing or worry.

Stacy said, "Are you guys the Keystone Cops or what? Why are you wasting time with us?"

Inspector O'Connor twisted his mouth into a faint smirk, his eyes still on Tess. "We know for a fact that Jake always travels with a female accomplice."

Stacy burst out in a great guffaw. "Ha, ha, ha." She shook her head and waved her hand at Tess. "Do we look the part? We just graduated from college two months ago."

The boss man grimaced and jerked his thumb up in the air. "Delaney, check the upstairs. Morris," he said, lifting his chin in the general direction of the front door, "check the perimeter of the building."

After the two men dispersed, O'Connor said, as if mostly to himself, "We'll get him. We always do." He then turned and began straightening the liquor bottles in front of the mirror, as though stalling for time.

"I don't think Jake is hiding back there," Stacy said.

Tess placed an elbow in Stacy's ribs and made a face at her, telling her to be quiet.

O'Connor looked at Stacy through the mirror, his eyes grinning. "That's very observant, Miss … What might your name be?"

Tess jabbed Stacy again in the ribs.

Stacy looked at Tess as one would an annoying fly. "I'd be Bonnie Parker, and this here is my sidekick Ma Barker," she said.

"Very funny, young lady, but—"

"I didn't appreciate getting strong-armed by your underling in the kitchen," Stacy said.

Tess grabbed Stacy's forearm firmly and said, "She's Stacy Enright, and I'm Tess Auld."

The FBI agent turned and placed his hands on the bar. "Now," he said in a demanding tone, "where's the bartender?"

Tess heard a tense bleat in her voice as she said, "He has the night off."

The inspector kept his eyes on Stacy. "And the owner of this place, who is he?"

"Tony Santini," Tess said.

"Toe—neee San—tinee," he said in a derisive tone of discovery.

Just then, the kitchen door swung open, and Tony walked in as if on cue. "What the hell are you doin' behind my bar?" He put both hands on the bar as if claiming his turf.

"FBI," O'Connor said, flashing his badge.

"Whadda you want?"

"We're looking for Jake Langeham. Where is he?"

"Got a search warrant?" There was a tone of controlled rage in Tony's voice.

O'Connor reached in his coat pocket, unfolded an eight-by-eleven sheet of bond paper with an official-looking seal and Search Warrant in prominent black letters. "Funny kind of place for a guy from Flatbush to be running." The FBI agent took a bottle of Chivas Regal off a shelf. "Unless he was washing big dollars through this very fine liquor." He raised the bottle toward Tony, as if producing exhibit A. "I hear this is Langeham's drink of choice."

"I ain't saying nuttin' until I talk with my attorney." Tony folded his hands across his chest and looked away from the agent.

Inspector O'Connor shrugged indifferently. "Have it your way," he said as he placed the liquor back on the shelf. A hard, dark look came over his countenance as he jabbed a finger at Tony. "But I am going to make your life around here, very, very difficult, Mr. Santini. You got that?"

Later that night, the girls went upstairs and found Teddy outside the open door of his room. "Somebody went through my stuff," he said.

Tess and Stacy explained everything, including Tess lending Jake one hundred dollars. "Oh man," he said, "I better check my stash of weed."

In his bathroom, Teddy drew back the shower curtain, stood on the bathtub wall, and opened the air vent in the ceiling. He reached up but found nothing. "When are they coming back?" he said to Tess.

Stacy came into the bathroom. "They ransacked our room too—the bastards."

"We might as well leave now," Teddy said.

"Why?" Stacy demanded. "I don't want to give those sons of bitches the satisfaction of running us off."

"Because," Teddy said in a determined voice, a new voice, "I had enough marijuana in this vent to ruin my chances of ever becoming a lawyer. And Tony's been laundering money for the mob through this place, and the feds will be closing it down."

Teddy secured the vent and stepped down. "I don't want to be answering any of their questions about any of this. I say we split tonight for our road trip."

They all looked at each other. In that instant, it seemed a lightbulb went on in their heads. They darted to their rooms and packed.

Tess tossed the last of the sleeping bags in the seatless back of Teddy's VW van. She paused for a moment and looked out past the cove at the blue-black sky aglitter with stars, the reflection of the moonlight shimmering over the water. She felt an adrenaline surge, like a convict scaling over a prison wall and disappearing into the dark of night.

"Ready?" Teddy asked.

Tess said in passing that she would never get her hundred dollars back from Jake.

"Wait here a minute," Teddy said. He went to the front door of the tavern and unlocked it with a key Tony had given him for emergencies. Tess and Stacy waited, looking around, half-expecting the roar of squad cars and the blare of sirens.

After what seemed forever to Tess but was probably only a few minutes, Teddy returned. "Here," he said, handing her five twenties. "I left Tony a note in the register explaining everything. Let's get out of here."

Chapter 3

ON THE ROAD

They drove in silence, Teddy behind the wheel, Tess sitting with her back against a couple of sleeping bags behind the front seats, facing the rear. Onto the Long Island Expressway, skirting north of New York City as they crossed the Throgs Neck Bridge through the Bronx, with still not a word spoken, Tess was on high alert for the inevitable flashing lights to pull them over and take them back to the Crockford in handcuffs.

Traffic was sparse, the headlights like ghostly entities, as they crossed the George Washington Bridge into New Jersey.

An hour after cutting across the Garden State, they entered Pennsylvania, where finally there was a collective easing of the tension that had hung inside the van since they left the Crockford. Teddy leaned back in his seat and exhaled. "Whew."

Stacy looked at Teddy and then turned back to Tess and said, "Those sons of bitches had no right to treat us like that."

Tess maneuvered around on her knees, gripping the two front seats. It was still pitch dark outside, with only an occasional oncoming or passing vehicle. "Let's keep on truckin'," she said.

"Absolutely," Stacy said, glancing at Teddy.

"Hell yes," Teddy said with a nod. "Once we get far enough west, we'll figure out an itinerary."

They drove on for a while with minimal conversation, as though collecting themselves, before Teddy told the girls that he had overheard Jake, earlier in the day, asking Tony for a loan. "Turned him down flat.

He told Jake that he had warned him about 'messin' with my girls,' and Jake still owned him money."

Tess asked how Tony knew about her and Jake. "I think it was more of a guess, but Jake didn't deny it," Teddy said. "Tony's smart that way."

Tess felt so used. Jake was a con man, after all, albeit a very fine-looking con man. She thought back to right before the FBI arrived and Jake had said, "What if ... kiddo." Was he going to ask her to come with him? Now she thought it mostly absurd, but at that moment, in that rush of exhilarated tension, sitting next to Jake and feeling that pull of attraction, she wasn't sure what she would have done. Left with him, hurt as she was about him bumming money? Tess could imagine her mother's reaction if Jake were arrested with Tess at his side, their pictures splashed across the front pages from coast to coast. "The Studly Gangster and His College-Girl Moll."

By the time they exited the Pennsylvania Turnpike into the parking lot of a diner in Hazleton, Tess had started to feel somewhat safer, and Teddy was once again laid back, but Stacy had been on a roll about the whole affair at the Crockford, "sons of bitches" strewing every other sentence.

As they took a seat at the counter, Tess told Stacy to forget the Crockford, that they needed to plan their trip.

"Yeah, yeah, I know." Stacy made a little gesture to indicate *one more thing*. "But it wasn't right the way *they* treated us."

"Turns out," Tess said, laughing, "the Crockford really was a crock."

"Uh huh," Stacy replied with an emphatic nod at Teddy, who was sitting between them, "the Crockford in Gatsbyville, my darlinks, a crock with a little *c*."

"Their historic tavern run by gangsters." Teddy put both palms in front of himself to indicate the obvious deduction. "Doesn't that make you two mob bimbos?"

"Damn, Mr. Bartender," Stacy said, "I sure hope so." She looked at Tess with a crooked grin. "I don't know about you, Tess, but *ever* since I was a little girl, it's been my dream to become a bimbo."

They burst out laughing. Let the road trip begin.

After they ordered, Teddy said, "I'll feel better when we have a couple of states between us and the Crockford."

The girls agreed, and they decided to take turns behind the wheel. Tess volunteered to drive since Teddy had driven the whole way from Long Island. "You and Stacy get some sleep. I'm good for at least four hours," she said.

So they departed Hazleton, with Tess behind the wheel and Stacy and Teddy, head to toe in the back, ensconced in sleeping bags. Heading west with a red-streaked dawn glinting in the rearview mirror, Tess felt an overwhelming sense of freedom as she drove up and down and through the granite mountains.

She had almost made a huge mistake with Jake; she saw that clearly now as she distanced herself from the Crockford and the pull of the Brooklyn lancer, Sir Jake, the con man. She wondered if it was something she needed to go through, an awkward step toward adulthood, and now her escape, Tess Auld sitting up high behind the wheel of a yellow VW freedom express. She wanted to bottle the moment of that exhilarating sense of anticipation that the road offered. It came over Tess that a new phase of her life was beginning, not just this trip but after. The last vestiges of her childhood were fading, and this trip would be a breaking away, a new beginning for the rest of her life.

By noon, a growing weariness gnawed on Tess, for she had not slept in over a day. She pulled off the turnpike into a service area.

As Tess filled up the van, Stacy came out and stretched her long arms over her head. "Where are we?" she asked.

Tess topped off the tank and put the gas nozzle back on the pump. "Forty miles from the Ohio line."

"Tess, you look dead tired," Stacy said. "I'll drive."

Tess snuggled into the sleeping bag behind the driver's seat. Teddy was stretched out on his back, with his head at the rear of the van. He looked so young and innocent, his chubby cheeks tinted light pink and the little snores whistling out of his lips that flapped ever so slightly. She was glad that even-keel Teddy was with them on this journey. There was a tranquility about him that was reassuring. And the easy, casual way he had gone back into the tavern to retrieve her one hundred dollars, Tess found it bordering on gallantry. She was seeing Teddy in a new light.

And she was seeing someone else in a new light—Buddy. She would do the honorable thing and drive to Denver and tell Buddy it was over.

Before departing the stop in Hazleton, Tess had called Buddy and told him to expect them in three days. Teddy was fine with Denver in three days, Stacy not so much. For some reason, she had never been a big fan of Buddy. But there had always been a tacit understanding between Tess and Stacy that they would visit him in Denver.

Tess turned on her side and felt a sense of comfort as the van lurched forward and then accelerated onto the highway. The sound of the tires on asphalt, the whooshing rumble of trucks they passed, and the comfort of the sleeping bag lulled her into a warm, deep sleep.

Tess had a dream where Jake had said right before his escape, "What if ... kiddo ... you come with me." She saw herself following him through a patch of woods at the rear of the inn and down a hill to a little bay, where a dinghy with an outboard motor was tied to a dock. She kept telling Tess in the dream not to do it, that he was a con man, but the dream girl said, "I love him," and flicked her hand as if to say, "Don't bother me."

Like a pair of fugitives on the run, Tess and Jake scurried on board the dingy, which Jake started up and drove out toward the deep water. "Kiddo," Jake said.

Tess turned her head back toward him. "Yes, Jake."

His hand was on the tiller, a cigarette dangling from the corner of his mouth, and his wavy hair ruffling in the wind. "How's Mexico sound?"

The whining sound of the van downshifting gears and the crunch of tires on gravel woke Tess. "No. No. Don't go," Tess mumbled in that half-awake, half-sleepy state. *What a dream,* she thought. She sat up and looked out the side window. They were pulling into a trailer park with a variety of mobile homes and campers. Teddy was back behind the wheel, and Stacy was sitting next to him.

Tess scrunched her head up to the front as Teddy pulled up to a permanent trailer on blocks.

"Hey," Tess said as she rubbed the sleep from her eyes, "where are we?"

"Miller's Trailer Park—Meadow Grove, Illinois." Teddy opened the driver's door. "Let me check it out."

Five minutes later, he returned with a legless, squishy cushion chair under his arm. "Bought it for two bucks," Teddy said as he tossed it in the back, "and paid four dollars for the night that includes use of outdoor showers."

After all three had cleaned up, Teddy drove directly to Big Annie's Bar and Grill. They sat in a booth, Stacy across from Tess and Teddy. The place had a honky-tonk quality with dim lighting, a jukebox, and various good old boys stationed at the bar. But the owner of the campground had told Teddy that they had the best burgers and coldest beer around.

After their pitcher of beer arrived, they decided to have a few cold ones before ordering dinner. The experience at the Crockford with the FBI was fading away in Tess's rearview mirror of time and distance. Jake was another matter. She couldn't shake off so easily the effect he'd had on her. Her dream of escaping to Mexico with Jake made that clear. *Give it time,* she thought as she took a long, thirsty swallow of beer. It was as cold as advertised and brought an immediate sense of relief, as though a release valve had been pulled.

Stacy finished her first mug in short order and poured another. "We need to give the van a name," she said.

"How about," Tess said as Stacy topped off her beer, "we call it something like the Yellow Freedom Express."

"That's close," Teddy said, tipping his glass as Stacy poured.

"I got it," Stacy said as she put the pitcher down, swishing the remaining contents. "The Mellow Yellow Freedom Express."

Teddy smiled and nodded. "Perfect. I now am the proud owner of the Mellow Yellow Freedom Express. Taking us away," he said, raising his mug as they clinked glasses, "from the tyranny of Big Brother and his FBI goons." All three burst out laughing.

Stacy, her eyes sparkling with her inimitable daredevil gleam, said, "I have always wanted to go to the Iowa State Fair, and it shouldn't be more than a day's ride from here."

This was all news to Tess, for in four years of college together, Stacy had never mentioned anything about state fairs.

"Stace, I already phoned Buddy. He's expecting us."

Stacy screwed up her face in mock disgust. "Buddy boy can cool his heels for a few days."

"I want to tell him I'm breaking up," Tess said.

"Well," Stacy said, "at least Jake served one useful purpose." She made a sweeping gesture with her hand, as though discarding trash. "Why not call him and let him know? I say we go to the fair."

Tess shook her head. "I owe it to him to tell him in person," Tess said.

Teddy squinted a look that suggested irritation, but soon his expression softened as though he had figured something out. "Let's kill two birds with one stone," he said. "How about we drop Stacy off at her fair, Tess and I go on to Colorado, break the news to the old beau, and we see the Rockies for a day, and then Stacy can catch a bus and meet us at the Denver bus station."

This was happening way too fast for Tess, but all she said was "How's that sound, Stace?"

Stacy shrugged. "Fine by me, but you guys don't know what you will be missing." She poured out the remaining beer in the mugs, slid out of her booth, and placed the empty pitcher on the bar. Stacy motioned to the bartender, a middle-aged, skinny guy with thinning hair and a world-weary look of someone who had spent most of his adult life behind a bar.

"Another pitcher," Stacy said, jerking her thumb over her shoulder toward their booth. "Also, where are your restrooms?"

All eyes were now on this tall outsider of a woman who acted as if she owned the place.

"Restrooms," said a querulous voice from the bar. "We call 'em toilets around these parts."

Tess held her breath, wondering what Stacy, born and bred in Dundalk, Maryland, and the daughter of an ironworker nicknamed Scrap-Iron, would do next.

Stacy shot a glance in the direction of the heckler. "Where I come from, we call 'em terlets," she said in her best *Balamer* accent.

The bartender pointed toward the end of the bar, and as Stacy made her way, the heckler swiveled around in his barstool and reached for her arm. She clenched his wrist and looked down at him. "Also, where I come from, it is not polite to touch a woman without her permission." Stacy put the man's hand on his lap as the other patrons roared with laughter.

"Looks like you had her pegged wrong, Larry," an old-timer at the bar croaked.

Tess looked at Teddy, who smiled back at her and said, "That's our Stacy."

After Stacy returned to the booth, the waitress brought over the pitcher and told them it was on the old-timer at the bar. Stacy filled her glass and raised it to the man. "Thank you, sir," she said. The man nodded and tilted his glass toward her.

After another pitcher and thick, juicy burgers and piping-hot fries, they drove to a country store and bought a Styrofoam cooler, bread, peanut butter, Cokes, and the like for their trip. By the time they returned to the campground, it was dark outside, and all three were tuckered out. They sunk themselves into their sleeping bags: Teddy, head at the rear, Tess and Stacy in the front. Within a minute, they were all sound asleep.

In midafternoon, they entered the city limits of Des Moines, traffic at a standstill. There was a festival attitude all around, with shouts and laughter coming from a gaggle of young people strolling down Main Street, which looked to be right out of a Norman Rockwell painting.

They were in the heartland, all right, for there was a wholesome quality from the low-tiered brick buildings with flowerboxes in windowsills to litter-free sidewalks to those clear-eyed good folks who crackled with excitement as they made their way to the fair. How different they were from the Waspy crowd and gamblers at the Crockford.

"Teddy," Stacy said from the back of the van, "you can let me off here."

A pickup truck was leaving a parking spot, and Teddy squeezed the van into it. Tess looked back at Stacy sitting in the cushion chair, long legs stretched out. "Stace, you sure? I mean about going off on your own."

Stacy stuck her head up front. "Of course, I am." She then dropped back and opened the sliding door. She grabbed her gear and said, "Don't worry. I'm a big girl."

Everyone got out of the van. Tess gave Stacy a big hug while Teddy stood by. Stacy then hugged Teddy. She drew back and offered a goodbye smile to Tess. "Not to worry."

"Don't forget to buy your bus ticket for Denver," Tess said. "Three days from now, we'll pick you up at the terminal." Tess knew she sounded like a mother hen, but she didn't want to get to the Denver bus station and not find Stacy.

"Don't fret, Tess," Stacy said. "Teddy boy and I have it all worked out." Stacy raised her hand in farewell.

As Teddy drove away, Tess turned back around and watched as Stacy, with canvas carryall in hand and sleeping bag strung across her shoulder, standing on the sidewalk talking with a group of college-aged kids. How fearless she was, Tess thought. As the van turned a corner, Tess's last image of Stacy was of her arm flailing over her head as she jabbered away, her long body animated with that limitless energy that drove her. Tess imaged she would have a place to sleep within fifteen minutes and by tomorrow would have made a new set of friends.

Outside the city limits, they came to a highway, and within a couple of miles, they were on the interstate. It seemed different to Tess, traveling without Stacy. It was just Teddy and her, and the dynamics of the journey had changed. She had sensed that when Stacy first mentioned her diversion, Teddy didn't like it, until it came over him that it would be just him and Tess. Tess wondered if he would have balked if she had been the one wanting to go to the fair and he was taking Stacy to see her beau.

In any event it, it would be Teddy and her showing up at Buddy's place to deliver the breakup news, which in retrospect had been developing since early summer, when Tess had a make-out session with a boy she met at a bar in Southampton. She had one too many shots of schnapps, and the next morning she regretted it deeply, and even more so when he showed up at the tavern after the lunch rush.

Teddy had picked up what was transpiring and introduced himself as Tess's boyfriend. The other boy studied Teddy for a moment, scrunched up his face with a look of utter disbelief, and said, "Bullshit."

"Ask Tess," Teddy said as he drifted his gaze over to Tess, who felt as though she were about die from embarrassment.

"He's not," Tess said, "but I have fiancé in Denver."

"Fiancé?" This guy had a nose for falsehoods.

"Okay," Tess said, "but we've been dating since my junior year."

"Denver is a long way from here," her pursuer said.

Tess now wondered whatever had she been thinking canoodling with this persistent pain. "Look," she said with a tone of finality, "it's not going to happen."

After the boy finally left, Teddy said, "You do cast a spell on them, Tess." There was a look of admiration on his face, a look of one seeing an expensive item that was out of his league.

By dusk, they were somewhere in the middle of Nebraska on a long stretch of prairie with an occasional farm dotting the landscape. They turned off onto an exit when they saw a sign for Gas and Eats. At an A-framed country store with one pump out front, an attendant of no more than twenty hustled out. Teddy told him to fill it up, and he and Tess used the restrooms. When they returned, the attendant was peeking inside the van while he filled the tank. "Road trip?" he said with a trace of envy.

"Yeah," Teddy said. "We're going cross-country."

The attendant topped off the van and inserted the nozzle back in the receiver. He offered a meek smile. "Wish I could take a road trip."

"What's stopping you?" Teddy asked.

The young man stole an admiring peek at Tess and then looked at Teddy. "Nothing, I guess. Never been out of Nebraska." He shrugged and then said, "That'll be $5.50."

"My turn to pay," Tess said as she handed over a ten-dollar bill.

"Where you folks headed?" the attendant said as he clicked out two quarters from his metallic coin changer around his waist and handed it to Tess along with four ones.

"Denver," Teddy said.

"The big city," the attendant said with a dreamy look.

"You know about any campgrounds around these parts?" Teddy said.

The attendant took off his St. Louis Cardinals ball cap and gave his head a thoughtful scratch. "No, but there's a motel down the interstate a ways."

"How far are we from Denver?" Tess said.

"Ah, you'd probably be all night on the road."

Tess looked at Teddy. "I'll take the first shift driving."

Back on the interstate, Teddy glanced over at Tess behind the wheel. "I wouldn't mind going to a motel."

Tess shook her head.

"If it's the money, I'll pay for the room."

Tess remained silent, her eyes straight ahead. Halfway up the sky to her right, a crescent moon floated.

Early the next morning, fifteen minutes north of Denver, Teddy took the Broomfield exit off the interstate and pulled into a group of garden apartments, with a backdrop of the snowcapped Rocky Mountains— how big and imposing they were. Tess got out of the van and breathed in the brisk air as a jangle of nerves came on her. She was going to break a guy's heart who had done nothing to deserve it. *Stay strong,* she told herself. They went to Buddy's door and knocked. Tess cringed as she imagined the look of surprise on his face when he saw them and then the look when she delivered the news.

Teddy knocked again, and they heard the jiggle of the chain lock and the door creak open. A tangle of Buddy's curly hair appeared first before he stuck his sleep-flecked face into the opening. When he saw them, his eyes bolted open, and his mouth gaped. "Tess, you're ... early."

Tess heard something or someone stirring in the background. "We drove all night, left Stacy at the Iowa State Fair."

Buddy stood there with a *huh* expression on his face.

"You going to let us in?"

"Well yeah ... sure." Buddy unlocked the chain and opened the door, standing there shirtless and in his underwear. Tess saw her from the corner of her eye lurching toward the bedroom in the back. She was in her panties and wearing Buddy's favorite flannel shirt, the one Tess had given him for his twenty-first birthday.

Tess felt a vague sort of sickness come over her as she stood in the hallway with Teddy at her side. Why this was, she wasn't sure, since she hadn't been true to Buddy. But it hurt to see that he had been shacking up with another woman.

Buddy sighed and said, "Look, Tess, you gotta understand. I got lonely."

"I came here to break up with you anyway," Tess said as she felt a conflux of emotion settle in her throat. "You just made it easier all around." She raised her hand in farewell. "Hi, bye, Buddy." With that, she turned and walked out of the building to the car, with Teddy alongside.

As Tess got in the passenger seat, Buddy came running toward them, barefoot, shirtless, and in jeans, pounding on the passenger door as they drove off. He was screaming at Tess, but she did not hear him. It was like a silent movie, in slow motion, Buddy's animated movements almost comical.

"What now?" Teddy said as Tess peeked in the side-view mirror and saw Buddy heading back into his building and to his awaiting Lolita.

Tess looked at Teddy and said, "You're going to think I'm crazy—"

"Let me guess," Teddy said. "You want to go back to the fair and Stacy."

She looked at Teddy for a reaction, but his look said for her to continue. "I went there feeling bad about what I was going to do to Buddy, and he beat me to the punch. I won't lie; it hurt a bit." Tess felt a swell of emotion flush her face. "It also seems that I am not who I thought I was for that matter. I need to be with Stacy."

"Okay, Tess," Teddy said as he slid a look over at her. "Not too worry. I will get you back there."

"Thank you, Teddy," Tess said. "You're the best."

They drove in silence for a while on the interstate, heading east, the sun rising through a bank of clouds.

When they crossed into Nebraska, Tess said, "Teddy?"

He glanced at her. "Uh huh," he said as he returned his vision to the road as a large semi whizzed by in the left lane. The road was not busy, but there seemed to be a preponderance of big trucks.

"Can I ask you a question?"

Teddy lifted his chin in the general direction of a billboard for the Burger Joint.

"Let's gas up and get something to eat, and I'll be all yours."

The restaurant was a small clapboard building with knotty pine walls and hardwood floors. They took a seat at a corner table next to a long window with a view of the Nebraska prairie. They both ordered burgers, fries, and a Coke.

After their drinks arrived, Teddy said, "Talk to me, Tess."

Tess looked out the window as a gust of wind blew tumbleweed across the landscape. It reminded her of an old western movie. "Do you think I'm screwed up?"

"No, you're just a very attractive woman who draws men like honey to a bee."

The waitress came by and said the food would be coming right up.

Teddy peeled the plastic lid off his drink and took a long swallow of his Coke. "If I had a girlfriend like you, Tess …" He looked up as the front door jingled open and two men in cowboy boots and jeans entered and took a seat at the front counter. He started to speak and peeked out the window before returning his gaze to Tess, his eyes so soft and brown and vulnerable. Just then, their food arrived and the waitress asked if there was anything else. "No thanks, ma'am," Teddy said. "Just the check please."

By the time they arrived in Des Moines, it was late afternoon. "Let's try the fairgrounds," Tess said. They parked on the outskirts of town and made their way through the endless maze of cars parked in various lots and along the perimeter of a huge campground with cars, RVs, and tents everywhere. Tess and Teddy suspected that Stacy might be staying there.

A few steps past the admission gate of the fairground, the sticky aroma of cotton candy and the warm fragrance of popcorn brought back childhood memories to Tess of an amusement park back home. But this place was so much bigger, with an array of circus-size tents and pens filled with massive, snorting pigs, mooing cattle, bleating sheep, and bellowing goats, food stands all about, and bands playing bluegrass or rock. The place was a bustling, noisy carnival, with the people casually dressed: many of the men in overalls or jeans; the women in shorts or pants, wandering about with children in tow; and loads of boisterous young adults.

They stopped at the Ferris wheel, where a long line of people was boarding. "Teddy," Tess said as she looked up at an elderly couple in a tottering seat at the top of the wheel, "we need to think like Stacy. Where would she go?"

Teddy thought for a moment and then said, "Wherever the most different and unusual event is."

They asked a great, burly, middle-aged man in jeans and a sleeveless flannel shirt that exposed tree trunks for arms. He looked capable of pulling a tractor out of a ditch. "Well …" He tipped back a straw hat, revealing a thatch of sandy-brown hair. "I reckon that'd be the butter cow."

After checking inside a tent where a life-sized replica of a cow was being sculpted in butter, they decided to walk around a bit, when Stacy came walking right toward them. What a sight she was. She had on bib overalls, her hair was spiked, and her two front teeth were blacked out.

At her side was a tall, gangly guy wearing thick glasses with a professional-looking camera around his neck. "Stacy!" Tess yelled and ran to her.

"Tess!" Stacy engulfed her like a long-lost friend.

They untangled, and Tess said, "Love what you've done with your teeth and hair."

Stacy exaggerated a smile and tapped her blackened front teeth. "Just trying to fit in with the country folk." She introduced Earl, a local photographer freelancing for a travel magazine. He was a good three inches taller than Stacy and built similarly, with broad shoulders and long arms and legs. He wore a ragged Grateful Dead T-shirt, jeans with a hole in the knee, and sandals—how perfect.

After handshakes and introductions, Stacy said, "What are you guys doing here, anyway?"

Tess needed to get Stacy alone and tell her about finding Buddy with the girl, to drink a couple of beers with her best friend and hash the whole thing out. But she sure as all hell didn't want to share it with this tall hayseed named Earl.

"I'll tell you all about it later," Tess said.

"Well," Stacy said, "how about we get you and Teddy set up with a tent at the campgrounds?" She looked up at Earl with a *what do you think* expression.

"Sure thing," Earl said evenly. "I've got an extra tent in my camper, and there's a vacant spot right next to our tent. Let's head back, and I can give Teddy a hand setting it up, and you girls can catch up on things." Earl glanced at Tess and then turned to Teddy. "Okay by you, Teddy?"

Teddy arched an eyebrow in Tess's direction.

Damn, Tess thought, *Stacy is already shacking up with this guy.* She nodded her head at Teddy to indicate it was okay by her.

"Sounds like a plan, Earl," Teddy said.

"Can we stop at the van first and pick up our gear?" Tess said.

"Let's go," Stacy said as she brought her hand up to her shoulder and pointed forward.

They exited the fairgrounds, with Stacy holding hands with Earl, and Tess and Teddy on either side of them.

After walking around the campground to the van and collecting the sleeping bags and change of clothes, they walked over to Earl's camper parked on the perimeter and got the tent and accessories.

Inside the campgrounds were rows and rows of tents of various sizes and even a couple of teepees. What caught Tess's attention was how orderly and calm everything seemed with such a mass of humanity. Folks were setting up grills and chatting amicably, introductions being made and handshakes all around. There was an we-are-in-this-together spirit in the air.

While Teddy and Earl set up the tent, Tess and Stacy took a seat on a pair of low-folding beach chairs in front of Earl's tent. Stacy ducked inside and came out with a cooler and handed Tess an ice-cold Pabst. "I figured you could use this."

So, between long swallows of beer, Tess proceeded to tell her tale of Buddy and his chickadee. "It surprised me how it stung to see that girl there," Tess said. "Even though I hadn't been perfect with Jake and all."

"Don't you worry anything about it, Tess." Stacy reached into the cooler and popped two more beers, then handed Tess one. "Let's just say, we've had one hell of a summer up to this point."

"Yeah, haven't we," Tess said half-heartedly. "I was still trying to digest everything with Jake—and then Buddy and that girl."

"Look at it this way, Tess," Stacy said as she slipped her hand on Tess's arm and leaned closer, "both of them in their own way revealed their true colors." She sat back and raised her can of beer, and they tapped rims. "You're better off without either of them in your life— especially Jake."

"You're right, of course," Tess said as she glanced over at Earl hammering a peg into the ground as Teddy watched. "But," Tess said through an emerging smile, "just like old what's-her-name at the diner said …" Tess offered a shit-eating grin at her best friend. "He was one fine-looking stud duck."

They broke out into muffled laughter, not wanting the guys to overhear.

Tess was already starting to feel better. "So, tell me about Earl."

"I met him at the stockyards taking pictures of a prize bull." She ran her finger around the rim of her beer and then looked at Tess. "I knew from the way he moved and the expression on his face that I needed a guy like him at this point of my life." Stacy took a swallow of beer and wiped her mouth with her forefinger. "And I tell you, Tess, it's nice being with a guy that's taller than me."

After setting up the tent, Earl and Teddy came over and joined them, each with a beer in hand. They sat on the ground facing the girls.

"So," Earl said as he cracked open a beer, "Teddy tells me I might possibly be associated with wanted fugitives."

"Oh, Teddy," Stacy said in an exaggerated dramatic tone, "I was waiting to get to know Earl better before … I told him about my sordid past."

"No, no, Stacy," Earl said, playing along, "I've been in need of a woman with a sordid past for some time now."

Everyone broke out laughing, none harder than Tess, who thought that this tall yank of country boy might be all right after all.

For the next two hours, they drank beer and ate burgers and hotdogs that Earl cooked on a small charcoal grill. And being back with Stacy, well, just like the incident with the FBI, Buddy was fading into Tess's rearview mirror. Jake, she was still working on.

Before they turned in for the night, Earl said, "Tomorrow, what say, we spend at the fair."

"Absolutely. I'm in," Teddy said, looking at the girls.

"You'll love it, Teddy," Stacy said, looking over at Tess for a unanimous vote.

Tess was silent for a moment, and in that silence, she recognized, as did the others, that she was still a bit off her game, one moment seemingly back to her old self, especially when it was just her and Stacy, and other times there were still some nagging sparks to extinguish. And then there was the one big question that would need an answer soon: was she losing Stacy to Earl?

Tess nodded her approval. "Wouldn't miss it," she said.

That night, inside their tent, Tess snuggled on her side, away from Teddy, who was lying next to her. She could sense his presence as though she could feel his mind working.

"Tess," Teddy said in almost a whisper.

"Yes, Teddy," she replied in tired voice.

"Oh, nothing … good night, Tess." Teddy rolled over, his back to Tess.

From Earl's tent, Tess could hear the soft murmur of laughter and then the not so soft grunts of sexual pleasure. Tess could feel it in her bones—Stacy was falling in love with this guy. The thought crossed Tess's mind that the loneliest sound in the world was other people, in love, making love.

After a while, it was silent in Earl's tent, a soothing, wrapped in each other's arms silence, and Tess wondered what hand, if any, fate would play in Stacy's romance.

Tess woke as a thin ribbon of light peeked through the tent opening. Teddy was still asleep on his back, breathing in and out in a gentle rhythm. He looked like a little cherub, a nice, sweet little cherub, cheeks tinted pink, long sweep of eyelashes, and ringlets of hair covering his forehead. She remembered what Teddy had said to her at the restaurant on the Nebraska prairie. "If I had a girlfriend like you, Tess …" He had stopped his train of thought, but the way he said it left no doubt about how he felt about her. She liked Teddy—a lot—but was not attracted to him.

Tess sat up and stretched. She had slept well and was looking forward to a day at the fair. She found Earl sitting in front of his tent in the lotus position, palms upward, resting on his kneecaps. His eyes were shut, and a barely audible humming sound was emitting from his mouth in intervals.

There seemed to be more to Earl than Tess's first impression of some yahoo farm boy. Not only did he have the right height for Stacy, but he had the same slightly warped sense of humor. This guy was no dummy, and he was assertive, someone who would stand up to Stacy's strong will.

The humming stopped, and then Earl's hands went out to the side and came together at chest level, not quite touching. He repeated this three times and then opened his eyes. He looked at Tess, his face expressionless for a moment. "Good morning, Tess." He squinted a smile and said, "I like to start my day with ten minutes of yoga." He shrugged and then lifted his chin toward Tess. "How did you sleep?" There was a chipper, *let us seize the day* quality to his voice.

"Great," Tess said. "Thanks for putting up me and Teddy."

"I like Teddy. You too for that matter." Earl smiled, revealing a gap between his front teeth.

Earl's tent opened, and Stacy emerged. She put her hands on Earl's shoulders, bent her long torso down, and kissed him on the cheek. "Good morning, sweet pea."

Earl smiled again, but this time it was more of a sideways leer, his eyes still on Tess. "First woman, ever, whose body fits mine like a glove." With that, Earl stood and declared, "Let's enter Stacy in the hog-calling contest."

"What?" Tess said. "She doesn't know anything about hogs."

Stacy put her hands on the sides of her mouth and let out, "Sooooey, soooey, here, piggy-piggy."

"Where did that come from?" Tess said, looking around, only a few people up and about.

"Damned if I know," Stacy said, "but I'm in—all the way."

The contest was held at one of the exposition buildings that was built along the lines of an elegant barn, painted a sparkling white and with decorative millwork and a stately cupola. Inside, a stage was set up facing rows and rows of folding chairs. Earl had signed up for this in advance and had turned over his entry to Stacy. On the way over, he had given her a few pointers. "Be loud, be confident, and snort for all you got." He let out a few boisterous snorts that sounded like short, choppy snores.

Stacy wasn't up for a while, so all four took seats as the competition began. It was a blast. Young, old, and in between gave their best sooey calls. The audience laughed but in a reserved sort of way, as though not wanting to let go completely—Midwestern reserve.

When Stacy's turn came, she went up on the stage, dressed in sandals, jeans, and a tie-dyed T-shirt that Tess had never seen before. She went to the microphone and raised it up a bit, cleared her throat, and let out, "Pigeeeeeeeee, pigeeeeeeee, here, pigeeeeeee, pigeeeeeee." She let out an uproarious snort like a heavy snorer gurgling a mouthful of water. Her performance lasted only a minute, but during it, her body was animated, as though an electric current were running through her. When she finished with a final, "Pigeeeeeeeeeeeeeee," the audience clapped, and even one man whistled his pleasure.

Earl said it was really good for a beginner, but she didn't have a chance of winning, so they left the hog-calling tent and wandered about the grounds. They rode the Ferris wheel, went inside the tents with enormous pigs and huge bulls, and ate corndogs, and all day they laughed and hollered and had a good old time. Earl was a country boy through and through but a lot of fun, and Tess could see that he made Stacy happy. Stacy could be moody, go off inside herself, and then just as quickly burst out into her old self again. But with Earl, she was riding a wave of bliss.

By late afternoon, they returned to the campgrounds, and all made use of the bathhouse and took showers. On the way out of the women's dressing room, Stacy said to Tess, "I'm going to be staying with Earl."

"Really?" Tess said as she felt something catch in her throat. This was her best friend, her Stacy, and now she was abandoning her.

They stopped and looked at each other, and in Stacy's bold blue eyes, Tess saw a glint of distance. Earl. He had, albeit unintentionally, come between them. At that moment, Tess knew it would never be the same.

When Tess first saw Stacy walking through the fairgrounds with Earl, the glimmer in her eyes, before she recognized her, said to one and all, "This is my guy." Down the road, who knew. No way could Tess see Stacy spending the rest of her life in Iowa. She had an unflagging enthusiasm for adventure, which a small town could not contain, to travel and explore and to meet new people and cultures.

So instead of fighting her on this, which would have been useless anyway, Tess said, "I'm happy for you, Stace."

"Thank you, Tess," Stacy said. "I hope this isn't throwing too much of a monkey wrench in the trip for you."

Tess wanted to scream, "I thought this was the last-stand Tess and Stacy road trip before all the BS begins!" But she only said, "It'll be fine."

Not having Stacy on the trip gave Tess pause. Did she want to continue on, with Teddy feeling about her the way he did? It could get awkward down the road.

That evening, they ate burgers and dogs again, compliments of Earl's grill. But this time, the food didn't taste as good to Tess or the beer as cold. No, everything about sitting in a low-to-the-ground beach chair with Stacy next to her, the two guys on the ground with legs crossed, sipping on their beers and gobbling down their food, seemed sad. She was losing Stacy and hadn't a clue when she would see her again. She was a little hurt that Stacy had chosen Earl over her. She knew it was crazy but couldn't help feeling that way, and also, Tess had to admit to herself, she was a little jealous that Stacy had found someone whose personality meshed so neatly with hers—two peas in a pod, Stacy and her sweet pea.

"So, I hear you two are hitting the road tomorrow," Earl said as he placed his empty paper plate on the ground next to him. He popped open a beer, took a long swallow, and let out an, "Ah, yeah, that hits the spot."

"Yes," Teddy said with a lift in his voice, "we'll be heading west." He looked at Tess, as did Stacy and Earl.

Tess knew she looked like she had lost her best friend—and she had. She started to speak but stopped, and suddenly a silence fell over the foursome as it became clear that Tess was not happy.

"Tess?" Stacy said. "Come on, you still have a great trip left to take." She nodded her head with emphasis. "The Mellow Yellow Freedom Express, no less." Stacy raised her eyebrows and opened her eyes wide, a happy, goofy smile splitting her face. "This might be your last chance."

Stacy was right, of course. Tess took a deep breath and nodded as if trying to convince herself. "You're right, Stace." Tess looked down at Teddy and smiled her angel smile. "Might be a little boring without Stacy along, but if you're willing, I am too."

Teddy put down his beer and clapped his hands three times. "Let's veer down to the southwest and visit New Mexico, Taos to be exact. I hear it's a cool place."

"I've been there," Earl said. "It's a different sort of place—hippies and art."

"How far is it from here?" Teddy asked.

"Ah," Earl said, "probably under a thousand miles." He raised a finger and said, "But it's all highway, and you could make it in one run in fifteen hours." He shrugged and took a swig of beer. "That is, if you were so inclined."

Chapter 4

TESS AND TEDDY

Tess woke at dawn. She peeked outside the tent, and there wasn't a soul about, everything still, only the chirp of birds rustling in the trees behind the tent. She and Stacy had said goodbye last night, since Teddy agreed to rise early and do the drive nonstop. There were a million questions Tess wanted to ask Stacy about staying with Earl. *What are you thinking? You just met the guy. Where are you going to live?* And on and on … but she didn't have an opportunity to be alone with Stacy, and even if she had, she would have held her tongue.

Hope you know what you're doing, Stace, Tess thought as she nudged Teddy awake. They had checked the map last night and would be driving right by Denver, which would have been a good stopping point. But Tess wanted nothing to do with being near Buddy's place.

Earl had told them last night about the interesting artwork and handcrafted jewelry that was sold all around Taos. In college, Tess had taken a couple of elective art classes and gone to a few bazaars where artisans sold their wares. The idea of creating something out of a blank canvas or a lump of stone had always appealed to Tess, though the only thing she had created were a few landscape paintings that her mother, who had started painting again after raising six kids, said were very good.

Tess had always had an interest in both art and making jewelry—she loved anything turquoise. She had a beaded turquoise necklace that she had left at her parents' house, not wanting to risk losing it on the trip. It had been a gift from her grandmother on her sixteenth birthday, and

Tess loved it at first sight. As her grandmother cinched the necklace around Tess's neck, she said, "You know, my dear Tess, that turquoise symbolizes self-realization."

An hour west of Des Moines, the sun, high and strong in a pale blue sky, let it be known who was in charge. It was going to be a scorcher of a day. So far on the trip, the weather hadn't yet been unbearable, but today would be different.

The van had no air-conditioning, and it was already getting warm, even with the windows down and the air vents open. They had agreed to take four-hour shifts behind the wheel, with Teddy going first. They were on the same road they had traveled back and forth to Denver, and it was boring and wide open. The speed limit was fifty-five, but Teddy kept it to just below seventy. "Gonna make it to Taos. We'll have to push it a bit," he had told Tess.

By noon, Tess was into her second hour behind the wheel, and it must have been nearly one hundred degrees. Wavy lines of heat appeared in the distance above the asphalt road. Tess flapped the back of her shirt to keep it from sticking to the tiny bubbles of perspiration forming on her back. She kept the speedometer at sixty-five, not wanting to push her luck.

As Teddy asked Tess how she was doing behind the wheel, she saw in the rearview mirror a line of blue smoke coming from the rear of the van. "Teddy, look," she said, leaning her head toward the rear.

Teddy looked over his shoulder and turned back. "Take the exit up here and let's find a gas station."

They were on the outskirts of Kearney, Nebraska, wherever the heck that was. It seemed like the middle of nowhere, a long, flat stretch of land. Tess remembered the gas station attendant in Nebraska on the way to Denver. He had a look of someone wanting to be anywhere than there but still couldn't pull the trigger.

Right off the exit ramp was a restaurant, gas station, garage combination. While Teddy went inside the garage to find someone, Tess went into the restaurant. It was a typical country diner with swivel seats at the counter, tables in the middle of the space, and booths along the perimeter. There were two middle-aged waitresses in light brown uniforms. A large fan in the back blew a breeze to the open screen porch's front door. Tess took a seat in a booth at the front window. Oh, what she wouldn't do for a cold shower right now. She wasn't hungry but ordered two chicken salads and large Cokes, "With lots of ice, please."

The waitress scribbled down the order, then said, "Where you headed, hon?"

"The Southwest." Tess didn't want to say Taos, figuring this big-boned, heavyset country woman, with a lined and wrinkled face of someone having lived a hardscrabble life, would not approve.

"Hotter down there," the waitress said before walking away.

The waitress brought the food and drinks, and still no Teddy. Tess idly sipped her Coke; outside, it was hot enough to fry an egg. The only thing moving were cars on the interstate off in the distance, appearing like a toy highway. Tony's finger-wagging warning back at the Crockford rose in Tess's mind like a bad dream. "If you break down in ... oh, I don't know, let's say Nebraska, where you gonna find someone to fix a Krautmobile?"

Tess had to laugh to herself. *Great call, Tony, great call.* As bad as this might be here in the middle of nowhere, with the van possibly kaput, she imagined Tony had much more serious problems to worry about with the feds.

Tess looked up at the creak of the screen door opening as Teddy came in. He spotted Tess and took a seat across from her.

"Well?" Tess said as she read the worry in Teddy's face.

Teddy pulled the lid off his Coke and took a long, thirsty swallow. He wiped his mouth with his fingers and said, "Mechanic is an old guy. Said he 'fought in Europe under Patton in WWII and *don't* work on Kraut cars.'"

"Wow," Tess said with a tone of disbelief at not only their predicament but also the irony. "I wish Stacy were here. She might be able to fix the van."

"We'll figure something out," Teddy said as he grabbed a fork and sunk it into his salad, "but first, let's eat."

After they finished eating, Teddy asked the waitress if there was anyone around those parts who could fix a VW van.

The waitress, who now had huge sweat stains under her armpits and droplets of perspiration on her forehead, said, "Where you kids from?"

"Back east, ma'am," Teddy said in a friendly tone. "You from here originally?"

Tess wanted to wring Teddy's neck, but then it dawned on her that he was trying to get on her good side.

After a couple of minutes back and forth exchanging life stories, the waitress sighed and said, "There is a fella who lives about five miles from here on a little patch of land that ain't worth squat. But he does side jobs on people's cars."

"VW?" Teddy said.

"He's a German—name is Krause. He also collects old VW vans." The waitress shook her head and made a sour face. "Lord knows why. They don't seem to be worth a plug nickel."

The inside of the van was like a furnace, the seats hot to the touch. Tess unfurled the sleeping bags and draped them over the seats. Teddy turned the engine over, and it sputtered to a cranky start. The waitress had written the directions on the back of a sheet from her order tablet. "It says to turn right out of the parking lot." Tess squinted to make out the writing. "After three miles, turn left on the dirt road."

So, off they went, the van sputtering and coughing its displeasure as they headed down a two-lane road.

By the time they got to the dirt road, the van was lurching and spitting out blasts of smoke from the exhaust pipe, like a belching chimney. "It says," Tess said, "Krause's place is one mile on the left."

It was a bumpy, dusty ride, but somehow the van managed to pull into a gravel drive that led to an A-frame clapboard house. Off to their right was a field with rows of old cars and more than a few VW vans, many just the shells. It was a rusted collection that reminded Tess of a graveyard for cars. Next to the house was a barn with double-wide doors opened wide.

As the van approached the barn, it groaned something terrible, and then the engine died—silence, a scary kind of silence in the middle of nowhere, no less.

"Oh boy," Teddy said. "I hope we haven't ruined it."

They got out of the van, standing there looking around, the relentless sun beating down on them. At the front door, Teddy knocked and knocked again but got no answer. They stepped off the porch and went over to the barn. Inside, there was a long workbench along a far wall, on both sides of which were shelves packed with auto parts. In the middle of the space was a car lift. They didn't see anyone. Then they heard the whine of a car engine and went outside. A VW bug came up and parked next to the van. A man with a shock of red hair emerged. He was huge—a good six foot three and barrel-chested with a protruding belly, thick freckled arms, and tree trunks for legs.

He was wearing black shorts, untied sneakers, and a white T-shirt. "Yah," he said at the sight of the visitors. He then went over to the van, walking around it, peeking inside. "It is yellow beauty," he said through a cheery grin.

"Mr. Krause," Teddy said as he and Tess approached.

Krause waved his hand in the air dismissively. "Just Krause," he replied in a strong, clear voice but with a pronounced German accent.

"The waitress at the diner down the road said you might be able to help. Our van was sputtering smoke, and then when we got here, it just stopped dead."

"Hah," Krause said with some force. "You lucky. I only one for hundred miles to work on this." He tapped his hand on the top of the van and then settled his gaze on Tess and nodded as if he approved. "Yah, let us get it in barn, and I take look later."

Krause and Teddy pushed while Tess steered, maneuvering it inside the barn. As Tess got out of the car, Krause motioned toward the outside. "Come inside my house. I have lemonade."

Tess wanted to ask if he couldn't look at the car now but held back. This man was their only hope, and she didn't want to upset him. Teddy, on the other hand, smiled easily and said, "That sounds great, Krause." He said it like they had been friends for years, Teddy and Krause.

The big German nodded his massive head in approval and shined a smile on Teddy, who replied, "I'm Teddy, by the way, and this is Tess." Krause looked at Tess with brow raised, his light blue eyes appraising in a not-unfriendly way.

The house was a typical farmhouse. There was a parlor on the left of the foyer, steps leading up to the second floor, a dining area on the right, and a kitchen to its rear, where Krause had gone to fetch the refreshments. But there wasn't a woman's touch about the place. The furniture was plain and utilitarian, and there were no flowers in vases or pictures on the walls other than a large painting in the parlor of a cobblestone village with snowcapped mountains. It was lovely and bespoke of another time and place. There was something sad about the artwork. There were people walking about, shop owners in aprons outside their establishments, but there was a quiet, forlorn atmosphere seeping out of the image, as if waiting for something to happen. Was it the furtive looks of the people or the mountains like giants about to engulf everything?

Krause entered the parlor with three tall glasses packed with ice and a pitcher of lemonade on a tray. He set the tray down on the coffee table in front of the hard-backed sofa that Tess and Teddy sat on. After pouring the drinks, Krause sat in a wing chair next to Tess, who kept stealing looks at the painting.

"It is my old village in Bavaria," Krause said.

Tess took a sip of her drink. "Oh, that's good lemonade." She looked at Krause. In his eyes, there was a look of remembrance. "It's wonderful," Tess said. "Your painting, that is."

Krause let out a stream of air like a long, low whistle. "My great-aunt painted it." He went on to tell how it was painted in 1910 in Paris, "before the world changed." He told of his childhood. "After the Great War, we were luckier than most in Germany, but then he ... that monster took charge."

Krause had served in North Africa during the Second World War. "I knew we were wrong," he said, shrugging, "but what could I do? Desert my country, my homeland?" He made a face that indicated that maybe he should have.

The big German went on for two hours while Tess and Teddy occasionally asked questions but mostly listened, his tone quiet, unhurried, and Tess found it soothing.

"What made you come to America?" Teddy asked.

"Hah," Krause said, "if you can't beat dem, join dem." He smiled a quick, devilish smile. "Isn't that what they say here?"

By late afternoon, the worst of the heat had passed, though it was still warm. Krause was wrapping up his life journey, having ended up in Nebraska after a failed marriage in New Jersey to a Polish woman. "I should have known better." He shrugged his enigmatic shrug and said, "No kids anyway." He had owned a VW car dealership and sold it and moved out here. "I liked the starkness of the land and the solitude of the people." He spread his hands above his head. "I buy whole caboodle, furniture and all. It seemed to fit my mood at the time." With that, he stood and said, "Let us look at your van."

Within an hour, Krause had the van running just fine. "It was nothing," he said, gesturing for them to follow him back to the house. "A clogged line, a sparkplug here, a sparkplug there." He threw his hands out to the side. "No problem. You are good."

"What do we owe you, Krause?" Teddy said on the porch.

Krause turned from the front door and made a face as if he had never heard of such a thing. "Nothing. Nothing at all. Thank you for your company and listening to an old man tell you about his life." Krause squinted a smile and said, "If you like, you can keep van here overnight and leave first thing in morning." His eyes made it clear that he desired company.

At this point, there was no way to make it to Taos unless they drove all night. Tess and Teddy exchanged a look, and Teddy said, "That would be great, Krause."

"Wonderful," Krause said as they stood in the hallway. "I have spare room, upstairs with bed for two." He kindly but shrewdly lifted his eyebrow in a silent "Okay?"

Tess was so hot and wrung out from the day's events, and without thinking, she said, "Thank you, thank you very much, Krause."

Krause nodded as though things were settled. "Room up steps on left," he said, pointing toward the stairs. "Shower stall outside on side of house. I leave you to it." His hands spread out a little to his side. "I make dinner for us."

Tess started to say something, but before she could, Krause raised his hand. "I never have guests," he said with a tad of emotion. "Allow me the pleasure of serving you dinner."

"Thank you," Tess and Teddy said in unison.

"It appears, Krause," Teddy said, "that we both agree. We would love you to prepare us a dinner and be your guests tonight."

"German dinner," Krause said. He then threw his hands in front of himself and said, "Go and shower, get rest. I will be in kitchen." He raised a cautionary finger. "And no helping."

Tess showered first in the outside wooden stall. She took it ice cold, and what a difference as she felt the tension and heat leave her. She dressed in shorts, flip-flops, and T-shirt, no bra. *Less is better,* she thought. Being in the middle of nowhere with this interesting man, Krause, and with Teddy alongside made her feel free and unencumbered. Tess was even looking forward to the evening.

She thought how Stacy would enjoy Krause's company and he hers. Why, she wasn't exactly sure, but Tess was partially glad Stacy wasn't here. Maybe it was because she liked the idea of being the only woman in the company of this enigmatic gentleman from Bavaria and, she also had to admit, Teddy. Tess had been impressed with how capably Teddy had handled himself today. He was definitely a people person. If it had been just her and Stacy at the diner earlier today, they wouldn't have befriended the old waitress the way Teddy patiently approached the situation. Teddy boy was starting to grow on her.

After Teddy showered, they went upstairs together to check out their room. They could hear Krause in the kitchen, singing with oompah-pah vigor in German. He sounded happy, like an entertainer at Oktoberfest.

Their bedroom was good size with a queen bed, dresser with mirror, two nightstands, and two windows with a view of the front of the house. Off in the distance, the endless flat land seemed to stretch to forever. Like the rest of the house, the bedroom furnishings were utilitarian. "The whole caboodle," Tess said with real cheer in her voice, and it came over her that she was coming around, Stacy's abrupt departure not so subconsciously omnipresent. Jake was definitely fading, and Buddy and his chickadee were long gone.

Teddy checked the closet and found a small fan and set it on the dresser and plugged it in. A whirring sound came from it, but it put out a strong stream of air. The room was warm but not unbearable.

"Are you okay sleeping in a bed with me?" Teddy said. He was looking out the window, his gaze on the van.

"If yah promise," Tess said in her best Krause accent, "to keep yah hands to yahself."

Teddy laughed. He turned from the window. "Not even cuddle," he said in a dead-on Krause voice.

"Funny boy," Tess said, "very funny boy."

Tess and Teddy peeked in the kitchen where Krause was cooking up a storm, steam rising from a pot of boiling water, large bratwursts simmering in a bed of sauerkraut, colorful vegetables in a colander. The big German turned, a look of bemused joy written across his even redder face. "You like beer?" Krause furrowed his brow, like an actor trying to draw a laugh from the audience. "I have good German beer. Strong beer." The brow lifted again.

"We love beer," Teddy said.

"Good, good." Krause made a sweeping motion with his hands. "Now off to the parlor, and I will come shortly with beer."

They sat back on the sofa, and Teddy slipped out of his sneakers and stretched out his bare feet. "Can you believe we're here?" he said, turning to Tess.

"It seems," Tess said in a low but assured voice, "we are in the hands of fate."

"And also a large gentleman from Bavaria," Teddy said through a grin, "with a penchant for fixing VW vans and cooking German food."

Tess slipped out of her flip-flops and stretched her legs out. "I love strong German beer." She looked at Teddy and raised her brow à la Krause.

"Yah," they both said at once and then burst out laughing.

After a while, Krause entered the parlor with three dimpled beer steins and a pitcher of dark amber-colored beer. He appeared to have cleaned himself up; his dark red hair was parted on the side, and he wore a T-shirt with Beethoven's face and name below, blue jeans, and sandals. "Here we are," Krause proclaimed as though he were presenting royalty.

He placed the tray on the coffee table and carefully and slowly poured a beer into a stein. He studied it for a moment like one observing a great work of art. He handed the stein to Tess. "Did you know in German the name Tess is short for Theresia, that is also the name of a volcanic island off Greece?"

"No," Tess said. "My Christian name is Theresa, but my little sister called me Tess, and it stuck."

Well, tonight, Krause said as he handed a beer to Teddy, "you are Theresia. *Tear as si ah.*"

"I am honored," Tess said with a slight bow of her head. She then took a taste of her beer. It was surely strong, with a hoppy aftertaste, but oh was it good. She took another longer swallow. *Let the night unfold.*

"Where you go tomorrow?" Krause said as he poured a beer.

"Taos," Teddy said.

"Ah," Krause said, nodding. "Taos different sort of place. Different sort of people." He let out a bellowing laugh. "Polar opposite of"—he threw his hands out to his side with a flourishing sweep—"around here."

For the next twenty minutes or so, they drank beer, the conversation light: weather, VW vans, RV parks in Taos that Krause had stayed at, and so on.

Soon, the pitcher was empty. Krause stood. "More beer?"

"Please," Tess said. "It is very good."

Krause returned in no time with another full pitcher. Beers were poured, and before Tess knew it, another pitcher had been emptied. "One more round before dinner," Krause said, not waiting for a reply as he swooped up the pitcher and left the room.

Halfway through the third pitcher, Tess was feeling bliss, the likes she could not recall. She was enjoying the company, Krause now fully engaged, telling stories about his childhood in Bavaria. "I yodeler as boy." He stood and took a deep breath, his massive chest protruding. "Little-old-lady-who. Little-old-lady-who. Little-old-lady-who."

When he finished, his guests applauded, Teddy letting out a shrieking whistle. And so it went, drinking beer and conversing with this unique man who seemed so out of place but at ease with his life on the American prairie. Tess did wonder if Krause didn't get lonely out here in the middle of nowhere, or if he found contentment and peace in this little nothing place. She sensed that in his life there had been some very difficult times during the war and after. But he never talked about it. Instead, he talked about his youth and his life in America, as though he had blanked out the bad parts. But behind the bonhomie, there was an edge of sadness that revealed itself in the gaps of silence—an inward look of reflection, as though his eyes were seeing long ago. It was all in his eyes, pale blue orbs that seemed to transmit something beyond words.

Krause topped off Tess and Teddy's beers, emptying the pitcher. "You sit. I will bring food to table." His tone was gentle but confident. "I call when ready. Not long." He then left the room.

By this time, Tess was feeling no pain. She glanced over at Teddy sitting next to her, who seemed about in the same condition. She placed her hand on his bare knee. "Pretty good beer, huh, Teddy boy."

"Great beer," he said as he put his hand on top of her hand.

Tess took Teddy's hand in hers. "You are a damn good road partner, Teddy. Damn good." Tess sensed that her words were a bit slurred, but what the heck—she was in good company.

Teddy slid himself next to Tess. She turned and looked at him, and their eyes locked. In that moment, magic fluttered about them: magic in the cooling air, magic in the personage of Krause, magic in this moment in time.

Tess leaned into Teddy and kissed him on the lips, her hand on the back of his neck. He brought his arm around her waist, their tongues suddenly inside each other's mouth.

Tess felt as though she were in an alternative world where there were no consequences for her actions. She had an urge to kiss Teddy, who looked so appealing, his dangle of hair draping his forehead, his infectious grin, his cutie-pie look. She had an urge to kiss him, and so she did.

"Dinner is ready." Krause's booming voice, from across the hall in the dining room, broke the moment as they untangled from each other.

The dinner was splendid. The brats and sauerkraut were moist and tasty, the German potato salad chilled just right to complement the warm brats, and a vegetable medley sprinkled in blue cheese. For dessert, Krause served apple strudel topped with a scoop of vanilla ice cream for his guests while he insisted on clearing the table.

When the last morsel had been eaten, Krause said, "Let us return to parlor for brandy." He looked at his guests as though to say, "Are you with me?"

"Why not," Tess said as she stood.

Tess looked outside the parlor window, waiting for Krause, while

Teddy sat on the sofa. The sun had sunk below the horizon as dusk settled over the land, the lone chirp of a cricket the only sound audible. Tess was still rather pleasantly tipsy from the beer, even after the big meal. She stole a peek at Teddy, who caught it and flashed a smile. Why had she not thought he was her kind of guy? Now that she was in this magical realm outside her normal world, he seemed mighty fine, mighty fine indeed.

Krause put the utilitarian tray, holding a bottle of golden-colored brandy and three thick tumblers, on the coffee table. He poured and handed them out. "A toast," he said, raising his glass. All three glasses clinked, and Krause said, "*Zum Wohl.* To your health." He then lifted his glass to indicate *drink*.

Teddy was sitting close to Tess, their legs touching, his bare arm brushing hers when he took a drink. Tess took a sip; it had a sweet, delicious fruity flavor.

"It is Obstwasser—apple and pear brandy. Good, no?"

"Yes," Teddy said in tone of surprise, as if he didn't think it would be so good.

For a while, they sat in silence, three people comfortable without words.

Krause turned on the lamp on the end table next to his chair, and it cast a soft glow of light into the room. Tess looked up at the painting of Krause's Bavarian village. She imagined herself living in such a world, so different, the pensive look on the people, the haunting mountains looming over all.

"Theresia," Krause said in a tone that reminded her of her grandfather. "I tell you story, before my time, about a girl in my village."

"I would love that," Tess said as she finished the last of her drink.

Krause refilled all three glasses and sat back with that sad remembering look. "She was beautiful," Krause said with a nod toward Tess. "The daughter of the village doctor."

"My father is a doctor," Tess said with a little shrug.

Krause nodded, his expression saying *but of course*. "All the boys in the village wanted to spend time with her, but her father was strict—no dating. One summer," Krause said, squinting, "I believe the year was

1886, she turned eighteen and went off to the Alps with her mother. By September, the mother returns but no girl."

Tess was leaning into Teddy, absorbed in the story but also feeling the charge of Teddy's awareness of her. She felt like she was in a fairyland, next to her a cherubic prince, listening to the wise, old German storyteller spin his tale and at the same time absorbed in each other's company, as though speaking a private, coded language.

"The girl," Krause said, staring at the painting, "all the boys wondered where the beautiful girl was. Finally, one had the nerve to ask the doctor, who only sneered and walked away. Finally, one of the boys' mother talked with the girl's mother and ..." Krause raised his heavy brow, took a swallow of his brandy, and smacked his lips. "The girl had met a young artist and wanted to run off with him to Paris."

Krause looked at Tess, a smidge of a smile in the corner of his mouth, the light eyes shining. "She told her mother she wanted to be an artist and travel whenever and to wherever she wanted. So ..." Krause said with a shrug and the raising of his palms like a preacher about to give the punch line to his sermon, "it seems this young woman had the call of the road." Krause then told a harrowing tale about how the girl's father sent out agents to bring her home, but with many circuitous routes, she managed to escape to Paris. Krause sat back, his brow raised, his eyes wide, and said, "And you know what her name was?"

"Theresia," Tess said, her eyes on the painting, "And she—your great-aunt—is the one who painted the picture on your wall."

A gentle breeze blew through the windows into the bedroom, and in the distance, dry lightning lit the sky. Tess turned off the fan and turned toward the bed, and there stood Teddy, those soft brown eyes smiling. He put his arms around her waist and brought her into him. "Tonight was special," he said in a whispery rasp.

After Tess's insightful identity of the girl in the story, Krause had looked at her and then the painting. "Very good, Theresia. Very good, indeed." From there they had another round of brandy, mostly in silence, as they all seemed to be letting the day and evening's events settle into their bones before all agreed to call it a night.

Now it was Tess and Teddy, all alone and together, his body soft and cuddly. Everything about Teddy seemed so right in this fairy-tale world.

She dismissed the little voice in the back of her head telling her there would be consequences for her actions. But right here and now, as they fell onto the bed wrapped in each other's arms, Tess wanted to live in the moment, consequences be damned.

Tess woke with a start. She felt groggy and achy and oh so hungover. She was lying on her side, trying to focus, and she realized that she was naked and, *Oh my God*, in bed with a naked Teddy. Last night came roaring upon her like a tidal wave. They had made wild passionate love—him on top and then the reverse, tongues licking body parts. Tess had let herself go with a vigor that she did not know she possessed. It seemed a stranger, an uninhibited stranger, had entered her body.

But now the fairy dust had worn off as she looked at Teddy lying on his back, breathing in his little gentle snores, lips parted in a happy little grin. *Now what?* she thought. Though he didn't say it last night, Tess saw it in Teddy's eyes. That look of romantic stardust.

Tess rolled quietly out of bed, the springs creaking—she wondered if they weren't creaking away last night—her departure. She dressed quickly and went downstairs. She heard Krause in the kitchen but went outside to the van, where she got a fresh towel before taking a shower in the outdoor stall.

She was beginning to clear the cobwebs as she came back into the house. Krause was in the dining room, fussing about the table with a bowl of fresh fruit, pitchers of milk and orange juice, and a glass container of cereal. "Good morning," Krause said.

"Hi," Tess said rather shyly.

"Hungry?" Krause said as if he already knew the answer.

Tess shook her head and smiled. "Thank you for everything, Krause."

"Ah," he said, "thank you for your company, Theresia." He raised his forearm and extended his index finger like a politician about to make a point. "In Taos, you visit the art galleries."

"I will," Tess said as she looked back to the pad of footsteps on the stairs.

Teddy entered the parlor, his hair disheveled, his eyes two squints of a late night, and a sheepish, happy-boy grin plastered across his face. Good mornings were exchanged, and then Krause said, "You have a ten-hour drive to Taos." He offered his hand for them to sit. "Eat some breakfast or at least a drink of juice, and I will bid you adieu." Krause forced a smile, but beneath it was that edge of sadness, of someone losing friends that he would never see again.

Chapter 5

RECONCILIATION

The drive to Taos was six hundred miles, and Teddy took the first shift behind the wheel. Breakfast with Krause had been quiet and not in the comfortable moments of yesterday evening, drinking German beer and later the golden brandy. Tess avoided eye contact with Teddy, and her mood seemed to pull a curtain of silence down on the meal. Last night in the otherworldly evening, Teddy had been so appealing and desirable, as though he were the only man in the world—her world of fantasy. She wondered if Krause had put some sort of spell on her—and Teddy to some extent also. She knew it did not make sense, but she could not shake the idea of how magical it all seemed, including the sex with Teddy—wonderful as it was. But she was back in the van and the unrelenting sun was beating down on the roof and windows, and Teddy, well, he now looked like the old Teddy, a nice guy, but the love interest had vanished along with last night's magic.

Now in the van, it was just the two of them—Tess and Teddy. Finally, Teddy broke the silence. "Look, Tess, about last night ..." Teddy looked over for some sort of reaction from Tess, but she remained silent. "We both had a lot to drink and ... well ..."

"Teddy," Tess said turning to him, "can we forget last night ever happened and go back to before?"

Teddy leaned his head toward Tess, eyes on the road ahead. "Go back to before," he said. "Yeah, I can probably do that." He passed a semi pulling a trailer full of wrecked autos. Back in the right lane, he glanced over at Tess. "But I will never forget last night. It was a special night, not only with Krause but with you, Tess. I will never forget that."

Tess wanted to explain what was going on inside her, but how could she? She wasn't sure what had brought it all on. "You're right, of course, Teddy; it was special." In the side-view mirror, Tess saw the semi fading into the distance with its damaged goods.

In the early afternoon, with Tess behind the wheel and Teddy asleep, stretched out in back, his head resting on the cushion chair, they approached the outskirts of Denver, Buddy's stomping grounds. It seemed a long time ago, her and Teddy's visit to Buddy and his Lolita. But it was less than a week. Old Buddy boy was really in her rearview mirror.

Tess and Teddy ate lunch at a diner off the interstate, and Teddy had more or less returned to his old self: a wry observation here and there, talking up the waitress like they were old friends, but it came off as trying a bit too hard, as though trying to prove to Tess that he could handle her rejection. She thought about whether she would take it all back, and no, she thought, for Teddy was right; it was special—all of it.

Chapter 6

WILD, CRAZY SHIT

By late afternoon, they had reached Taos. The heat and humidity had subsided, and in its place was a warm, semiarid feel in the air. Teddy was back behind the wheel and heading toward a campground Krause had mentioned as suitable and inexpensive.

"Look at that," Tess said, pointing off to her right. In the distance, golden-brown mountains shimmered in reddish hues in the fading sunlight.

"Taos Mountains," Teddy said. "Krause said the campground is at the base."

Tess liked everything about New Mexico: sagebrush covering the rugged terrain, a hot-air balloon soaring by, and the town of Taos, everything neat and orderly as they drove past galleries displaying artwork in their front windows and shops selling beads and jewelry. A collective hum of energy permeated this town of adobe and stucco buildings, a creative hum of free-spiritedness, as people were walking about to and fro, some of the women and long-haired guys in cutoffs and sandals. Tess figured these folks were artists or hippies or maybe both.

A few miles past town, they came to a pueblo village. Teddy said he had read about it and asked Tess if she wanted to look around before heading to the campground.

"Absolutely."

To their surprise, there was an admission fee that Tess insisted on paying for. The adobe buildings were built side by side, two of which were five stories high, supported by large timbers, and the interior white walls were clean and bright. There were shops inside the pueblo selling artwork, jewelry, pottery, and the like.

"This place was built over a thousand years ago and is the oldest continually inhabited community in the country," Teddy said as they peeked inside a curio shop. In front of a wall with an impressive display of silver and turquoise jewelry was a woman dressed in a breechcloth with leather leggings and moccasins, her thick, dark hair in braids. A jade and turquoise bracelet caught Tess's eye. She went over for a closer look. It had a simple yet lovely design of adobe huts backdropped by the turquoise.

"It is a storyteller bracelet," the Indian woman said to Tess. She was in her midforties, heavyset, yet her face was smooth and unlined, her skin a creamy tan, and her dark eyes held Tess's gaze in hers. "It is a legend for many generations of Navajo people."

"It's beautiful," Tess said.

"Try it on," Teddy said.

Tess looked at Teddy and then the woman, who nodded okay.

Tess placed it around her left wrist, and it fit perfectly, as if it belonged there. She lifted her arm and turned her wrist. She loved it. "How much?"

"One hundred and fifty dollars."

"Oh," Tess said as she took the bracelet off and placed it back on its hook.

"Put it back on," Teddy said as he pulled out his wallet and handed the woman the money.

"Teddy," Tess said in a low, sharp voice, "I can't let you pay for this."

Teddy nodded a thank-you to the woman, who handed him the bracelet. Teddy took Tess by the arm and guided her outside the shop. "Look, Tess, my old man is loaded. I'm on a generous allowance, plus what I made at the tavern." He handed her the bracelet. "It's a storyteller bracelet." He paused, considering. "It seems this trip we're on is sort of a story in itself." Tess started to speak, and Teddy raised his hand. "It would not seem right for you not to have it."

By dusk, they entered the campground, which was a barren expanse of hard-packed desert floor, with a few RVs and camper trucks parked about. There were picnic benches and stone grills located in a tamped-down gravel patch, and there were restrooms and showers under a timber pavilion. They parked next to an old, gray, dinged and dented Chevy station wagon, in front of an adobe structure with a faded brown terra-cotta roof. Out front was a wooden placard—Handlebar's Campground.

At the front door, Teddy started to open it, thought better, and then knocked. A tall, gaunt figure of a man, with a bushy mustache, which slanted down the sides of his mouth, and salt-and-pepper hair in a ponytail, answered the door.

"Howdy," the man said.

"Hi," Teddy said. "We're looking to rent a spot for my VW van."

The man asked them to come inside. Along the back wall was a loft with a handcrafted wooden ladder as access. The floor was hardwood, the stucco walls adorned with metallic works of art with a varied array, from a painted smiling sun to a howling coyote. A small countertop with two stools separated the small kitchen off to the right, the office counter and desk on the left, and the living space in the back with Adirondack chairs and a wooden bench with cushions. There were two large skylights in the roof. The place had a cavernous yet welcoming quality.

The man went behind the office counter, producing a three-ring notebook. "Ah, let me see what I got for you," he said as he flipped through the pages and stopped. "Here we go," he said, tapping his long, gnarled finger on the sheet. "Number 16." He looked up and smiled, revealing a dark, gummy hole in place of a missing canine. "Twenty-five a week or five a day." His tone was breezy in a matter-of-fact sort of way.

Teddy looked at Tess, who made a face to indicate she wasn't sure.

"Can we …" Teddy said, "do five a day for now and still have the option for a weekly rate?"

"Well …" the proprietor said as he ran his thumb and forefinger down the sides of his mustache, "I reckon for a few days that will be all right."

They paid for two days and registered, including showing ID. "Just to make sure you are who you say you are," the man said. "My name is Winslow, but everybody calls me Handlebar." He grinned his gummy grin.

"Sort of figured that might be what you go by," Teddy said.

Handlebar looked down at what he had just written in the register. "William Van Hollen and Theresa Auld," he said, looking up. "Those are a couple of righteous names."

"I go by Tess, and he's Teddy."

Handlebar pursed his lips and said with an emphatic nod of his head, "Tess and Teddy. Got a good ring to it."

Number 16 was at the end of a row that was occupied by a silver Airstream toward the front, an RV in the middle, and a heavy-duty pickup truck, with a jury-rigged camper atop the bed, situated across the row from them.

Tess and Teddy were both tired after a long couple of days on the road and decided to eat in the van and then turn in for the night. Tess made peanut and jelly sandwiches. They ate in the front seats, looking out at the mountains in the distance, Taos in the foreground glittering like fireflies hovering over the terrain. The moon hid behind a cloud, giving off a muted light in contrast to the black sky looming over the mountains.

Teddy took a bite of his sandwich and washed it down with a long swig from a can of Coke. "We've come far," he said in a remote voice, as though only part of him were there.

Tess watched the moon peek out from behind the cloud. "Are you okay about everything?"

Teddy kept his eyes on the vista in front of him. "Yeah," he said through an emerging grin, his Teddy-boy grin. "I will *always* have last night to take into my eternities." He looked at Tess, and they both broke up into hooting laughter.

Tess woke first, her head at the front of the van, Teddy's at the rear. She had turned in first last night. Teddy had said he wanted to sit up front and read for a while. He had a dog-eared version of *On the Road*, the iconic road trip story by Jack Kerouac. Tess wondered whether he was trying to make it less awkward—the first night after.

Tess carefully climbed in the front, trying not to wake Teddy, and went out the passenger door. There was a coolness in the air as she stood barefoot in shorts and sweatshirt. She had slept well last night and felt refreshed, as though beginning on a clean slate. Over at the pickup camper, a man sat in a lawn chair, coffee mug in hand. He raised his hand toward Tess and said softly, "Good morning." He was middle age, an Indian, Tess figured by his high cheekbones, strong aquiline nose, and brown skin.

Tess raised her hand and smiled hello.

The Indian raised his mug as if offering her a cup.

Why not, Tess thought as she walked over.

"How do you like it?" the man said as he stood and offered his chair to Tess.

"Black is fine."

The man went into the back door of the camper and soon returned with a steaming cup of coffee and another chair.

He handed Tess her coffee, unfolded the chair, and sat. "Nothing like the high desert in the morning."

Tess took a sip of her coffee—it was hot and strong.

"If that don't open your eyes, nothing will," the man said. "Name is William Half-Moon." He offered his hand to Tess, who shook it. His grip was firm, his hands calloused.

"Hi, William. I'm Tess."

They chitchatted for a bit, exchanging where they'd been. William was traveling solo, wherever the back roads took him. He had spent twenty-five years as a policeman on an Indian reservation up in North Dakota, and this was a retirement gift to himself. "No family, other than some no-account cousins on the rez," William said. "Met some interesting folks traveling across this great land." He looked up as Teddy approached. "Coffee?"

After introductions, William came out of his camper with another chair and a coffee. Teddy asked William if he knew what to see and do in Taos.

"Planned on staying for a couple of days, but been here nearly a week." William shook his head and smiled. "This place grows on you." He mentioned a couple of bars, "for the younger crowd," and where to find the best deals on artwork, "if that's your thing." He also mentioned a commune of people, "Some old-time hippies and younger folks like yourselves," that were totally self-sufficient. "I hear from Handlebar that all types of shenanigans go on there." William's eyes grew wide, and a mischievous smiled creased the corner of his mouth. "Not that I'm opposed to that sort of thing."

Tess and Teddy spent all morning in town, wandering in and out of the low adobe buildings in earth-tone hues, looking over a variety of art and handcrafted items. There were people of all types, all seeming to possess a live-and-let-live persona: men in blue jeans and cowboy hats driving battered pickups, folks of all ages and in all types of clothing from the raggedy hippies to the upscale, well-dressed folks. Some of the hippies had a cultivated look that that even their tie-dyes and sandals and long hair couldn't hide completely. They reminded Tess of some of the bluebloods at the Crockford but dressed down and with a scruffy makeover. The older artists, especially the women with their gray hair falling freely down their shoulders, had an aura of independence about them, as though they had found their true bliss.

At Taos Plaza—a lovely open space of shops and greens and a courtyard with a gazebo—they ordered carryout at a Mexican restaurant and sat on a bench under a leafy tree. "After we eat, let's drive around and see what we see," Teddy said as he reached into the carryout bag and handed Tess a taco and lemonade.

Back at the van, a school bus painted in bright psychedelic patterns with no discernible rhyme or reason was parked in front. "Hippies," Teddy said in an amused tone of discovery.

They went up for a closer look. Tess stood on the curb, peeked in an open window, and smelled the faint aroma of marijuana. The seats were gone, and a few boxes and crates occupied the space.

"Find what you're looking for?"

Tess and Teddy turned to see a man in his early thirties, in a dark T-shirt, cutoffs, and sandals. He was of medium size with a lean, wiry body, bits of paint on his hands and arms.

"Hi," Teddy said. "Let me guess. Artwork?"

"Very good," the man said as he smiled. His hair was curly and blond, and his face looked Nordic, all angles as though chiseled. He turned his attention to Tess. It seemed he had somehow determined that they were not a couple but more friends. It was in the unguarded way he looked at Tess, the piercing blue eyes smiling, flirting more than a little. There was something wary and at the same time charming about him.

"What type of art?" Tess said.

"Variety," he said. "Landscape, portraits, and then your wild, crazy shit." He flashed a wicked smile, his row of even white teeth like large pearls on a string.

Tess took Teddy's hand in hers and said, "Are you from the artist community we heard about?"

"Yes," the man said, his gaze still tauntingly sexual.

"My girlfriend and I," Teddy said as he put his arm around Tess's shoulder, "have always wanted to see what one was like." There was a slight tone of *nah, nah, nah, nah, nah* in Teddy's voice. A voice that said, "She's mine, and you can't have her."

"Stop by this evening," the man said, "and check it out. We're having a bonfire." He held out his hand to Tess. "By the way, I'm Wolf."

Tess leaned back a little, appraising.

Teddy reached over and shook Wolf's hand. "Wolf," he said as if he were playing with house money, "I'm Teddy, and this is Tess." He paused and glanced at the bus and then back at Wolf. "We look forward to some wild, crazy shit."

After departing Taos, with written directions from Wolf, Tess and Teddy browsed at another Indian pueblo village similar to the one where Teddy had bought Tess her bracelet, and then they drove around the countryside. Tess liked everything about this region of the country: the dry, arid climate, the rough yet hauntingly beautiful high desert landscape—6,967 feet elevation according to a road sign—and the creative spirit that seemed omnipresent.

They bought some apples at a vegetable stand on the side of the road, where an old woman with snow-white hair and a seen-it-all look was the proprietor. She had lived in New Mexico all her life. "I lived in an artist community back in the twenties," she said with a crinkly twinkle in her eyes. "Nothing those youngins doing today that we didn't do."

Heading back to the campgrounds, Teddy stopped at a country store and bought two six-packs of beer and ice and filled a Styrofoam cooler. Pulling into the campground, they saw Handlebar and William sitting in front of William's camper, sharing a joint.

William hollered for Tess and Teddy to join them.

Teddy grabbed the cooler, and by the time they got over, William had arranged four chairs in a circle. After the joint was passed around, Teddy handed out beers.

"That's good weed," Teddy said as Handlebar offered him another toke.

"Maui Waui," Handlebar said.

A comfortable silence fell over the foursome. Finally, Teddy said, "Tess, what you say we pay Handlebar for a week?"

"That'll work," Tess said as she looked off at Taos Mountain, shining russet and earth tones in the late-afternoon light. It seemed close enough to reach up and touch.

Teddy told about his and Tess's day and the invite to Wolf's commune. Handlebar mentioned that he had never been there. "Though I have driven by the entrance. Suppose to be some wild things going on there."

"Let's all of us go," Teddy said. "Let's drink a few more beers and see what's what with Mr. Big Bad Wolf and friends."

"I'll drive you in my gray ghost," Handlebar said, lifting his chin in the direction of his station wagon.

Around five miles from the campground, they came to a dirt road on their left. At the entrance were two stone pedestals with an arched sign of wood fibers that spelled out Eros and Psyche's Secret Palace. "Hah," Handlebar said as he looked at William riding shotgun. "Now we're talking."

Less than a mile down the windy lane, they came to a jut of land. Off to their left was an open pavilion of canvas on poles. Further back was an A-frame structure, and off to the side and behind it were similar but smaller shacks. In an open space in the front of the property was a stone pit with long, thick logs stacked pyramid style. Handlebar parked off to the side of the road behind a line of cars.

Clusters of people were talking and laughing. There was a joyous, liberated sound to the voices, as though they hadn't a care in the world. They were mostly from early twenties to midthirties, and some of the younger women were topless with bright-colored body paint covering their bodies, including their nipples. "Damn," Handlebar said as they walked up, "now, this ain't half-bad." He took a deep inhalation. "That smells like some good hemp." He looked at William, who took it all in with a slanted look of appraisal.

The whine of an engine and shifting gears of a large vehicle drew Tess's attention to her rear. Here came the psychedelic school bus. In the dusky light, Tess couldn't make out the driver, who parked behind Handlebar's station wagon. The door shushed open, and Wolf hopped out, wearing a red bandana around his head, a fat doobie behind an ear. He was shirtless, and his body had a fit, hard musculature. "Well, well," Teddy said as Wolf approached, "if it isn't the Wolfman himself." He said it loud enough for Wolf to hear.

"Welcome," Wolf said, ignoring the comment. "I see you brought guests." He nodded his approval. "The more, the merrier." Two topless girls in cutoffs came up to Wolf, and they engaged in a long group hug, arms around shoulders.

"How did it go in town?" one of the girls asked Wolf. She had dark brown hair, a well-formed, pretty face, and large, firm breasts that Handlebar kept stealing glances at.

"Sold five paintings, including *The Mad Hatter*. Well done, Vicky. Well done." Wolf's tone was that of proud mentor. But in his eyes, there was a flirtatious, knowing gleam.

"Yay," the girl said, clapping her hands in little rapid pats. She looked at the other girl—blonde, shapely figure, and written in red, swirly fonts below her navel was *Pussy's Home*. "Sara," Vicky said to the blonde, "I am an artist." She lifted her hands over her head and then grabbed the other girl's hand, and the two of them pranced off as if they were strolling down the Yellow Brick Road.

Wolf smiled and shrugged at his guests. "We have wine," he said, lifting his chin over toward the pavilion, "and of course plenty of weed." He removed the joint from his ear. "Anyone have a match?"

Handlebar pulled a lighter from his pocket and lit Wolf up.

Wolf took a deep, long drag and then passed it to Tess.

William was last and took a slow but steady inhale. "That's some very fine stuff," he said to Wolf, handing it back to him.

"Homegrown," Wolf said. He spread his hands out to his side and said, "Enjoy, wander around, check things out. Bonfire at nightfall." He then walked off.

This surprised Tess, who expected Wolf would try to make some sort of move on her. Part of her was a little miffed, and that surprised her.

By the time Wolf lit the fire, the mountains were a black outline against a starry sky. He seemed to be the head honcho: flitting around, talking, flirting, big-personality guy. He reminded Tess of a hippy version of Tony back at the Crockford. How long ago that all seemed.

William and Handlebar had wandered off with a couple of women who appeared to Tess to be close to forty. Both women were thin with sharp features, a bit of a puckered country look hovering about their faces, as though they at one time would have fit right in on the front porch of an Appalachian cabin. One wore a headband of dandelions, and the other wore one around her neck.

Tess and Teddy were at the pavilion drinking wine from plastic cups. Inside was a long table made of logs, atop which was an oak bucket filled with homemade wine, which Tess found a little tart but not bad. People were not moving about as much as earlier, as the effects of the wine and marijuana had taken hold, including Tess, though she was still a bit wary about all that was going on around her.

She didn't like to think of herself as conservative like her parents, but seeing these half-naked girls had been a shock to her. Tess couldn't imagine ever doing such a thing. Tess and Teddy had a few conversations with some people, who all seemed a little too friendly to Tess, as if they were trying a bit too hard to get into the role of hippy. "Boddie asked me to do it in the road with him," one girl of no more than twenty said as general conversation to a group that included Tess and Teddy. She reminded Tess of an actress auditioning for a role, an untrained one at that.

Another girl approached them and said to Tess, "Can I borrow your old man?" She was in her early twenties with flowing blonde hair, topless—of course—with nary a drop of paint on her body that had curves and rises in all the right places. She seemed very proud of her physical attributes—a confidence in strutting around showing off her gorgeous breasts with large nipples adorned by a ring of areolae like perfectly formed satellites around the mother planet.

"He's free to speak for himself," Tess said as she glanced at Teddy standing next to her, mouth gaped slightly open and his eyes wide as if to say, "What I have fallen into here?"

"I'm Teddy," he said with one of his Teddy-boy smiles.

"I'm Tess," the girl said.

Teddy threw his head back, mouth opened in full uproarious laugh mode but nary a sound, like a character in a silent movie. He looked at Tess, his brow raised. *Can you believe this?*

Tess knew she had no right to say anything against whatever this girl had in mind with Teddy, but ...

"I would love to be borrowed," Teddy said as he reached for her hand and walked off with her into the dark of night.

Did this girl also think that Tess and Teddy were not a couple, or did she not care if they were? It was different, Tess thought, to be on the other side of this paradigm.

By this time, the bonfire was ablaze, and Tess went out to get a closer look. Sparks flew up into the darkness, only to suddenly die out as the fire crackled and roared, emitting a tremendous amount of heat. Tess stepped back from the heat and right into a hard, firm body. She turned, and there was Wolf, with a *where have you been all my life* look across his face. "Love that bracelet on your wrist," he said.

Tess unconsciously touched the bracelet. Caught off guard by his sincerity, she wondered if the artist side of him was emerging.

"May I show you around?" Wolf said, holding his hand out to Tess.

She noticed his fingers were long and supple, and his hand gave the impression of sinewy strength though it was somehow delicate. Tess took his hand in hers.

They entered the main building in the center of the commune. Inside were workbenches along the side walls stocked with canvas rolls, picture frames, jars of paint, and spray bottles. Along the back wall were different styles of artwork on easels in various degrees of completion.

"Let me show you what I do," Wolf said.

In the back corner was a modern painting of a woman's head and neck and shoulders, elongated and tilted at an angle, surrounded by lines and blocks of subtle pastels. A hand—her own?—ran up the side of her face. There was something deep and intriguing about this piece of work. "I like it," Tess said. "It could be interpreted in different ways. To different people, she's looked at differently." Tess turned to Wolf for confirmation.

Wolf nodded his approval, and his expression that had seemed so arrogant and strong-willed now drew into itself. "You have the eye of an artist."

They walked about the property, which certainly appeared to be a self-sufficient community: stone fireplaces, with warming ovens here and there; a slanted-roof henhouse painted bright red, with twenty or so roosting chickens clucking contently in straw beds; and a well with a metallic storage tank near an impressive garden with rows of green plants and tomatoes.

At the back of the property were two outhouses, like tiny log cabins.

On the way back, Wolf stopped at a small adobe structure. "I built this myself," he said in a matter-of-fact tone. He opened the door and looked at Tess, who hesitated for a moment. She was still under the influence of the marijuana and alcohol. One voice whispered in her ear, "Don't go there in your condition and do something you will regret in the morning." The other voice said, "What will it hurt to look? This is your great adventure. Don't chicken out now."

Tess stepped inside. The space was basic yet comfortable looking. On one of the plastered walls was a chalk mural of mountains and desert. It was done in earth tones and subtle colors like the painting of the woman.

Tess leaned in to get a closer look. "Is that a wolf?" In the background was a faded, ghostly black doglike figure loping across the desert floor.

"My doppelganger," Wolf said. "Do you know what that is?"

"No," Tess said as she took a closer look, "but I think I see the connection."

"Of course you do," Wolf said in an assured tone. "You see things." He looked at Tess with solemn intensity.

Tess turned from the painting and Wolf's gravitational pull to check out the rest of the living quarters. Against the back wall was a large bed, covered by a quilt, with a motif of star pattern and feathered headdresses, anchored by a bed post made of interweaving tree branches. A bookshelf along a wall was packed with paintbrushes, sketchbooks, drawing boards, and the like. Another shelf fastened to the wall had a line of thick books, such as *The Story of Art, History of Western Art …* The only furniture was a paint-stained drafting desk and a rumpled and worn loveseat.

Wolf offered a hand for Tess to sit on the love seat. He sat next to her but kept a gap of space between them. "I have a request," Wolf said, looking at her with his artist's eye. He wrapped his fingers around the bracelet on her wrist, his touch strong yet gentle, warm and inviting.

Wolf leaned toward Tess, his face in hers, his eyes searching hers. She didn't move, and a rush of desire overcame her as he kissed her on the lips.

Tess drew back and took a breath. "You said you had a request."

"Yes," Wolf said in a more formal voice. "I would like to paint you. Nude."

Just then, the front door banged open, and the two topless girls, Vicky and Sara, last seen figuratively cavorting down the Yellow Brick Road, burst in. Sara, the blonde, had a joint dangling precariously from her mouth, and Vicky was now completely nude, her body paint smeared, as was Sara's. A jungle of dark pubic hairs covered Vicky's crotch, bringing to mind some wild, untamed Amazon.

"When are you going to paint me, Wolf?" Vicky said in the voice of a pouty little girl who always got her way.

"Why don't we," Wolf said standing, "share Sara's joint and then discuss an idea that has come to me." The sharp angles had returned to his face as the jaw jutted out, and the body stood erect and rigid as though he were imitating a statue. It seemed this man, this artist, had many guises.

The little voices were back in Tess's mind—one saying to get out, the other advising to listen before doing anything rash. She stayed seated as the other two girls sat on both sides of her. Their bodies were moist with perspiration, exuding a spongy, tangled sheet sort of odor.

The joint was passed around, and Tess took a toke.

"What's your plan?" Sara said in a singsong voice. "Well ..." Wolf said as he took a long inhalation, his chest expanding as though filled with helium before exhaling in a long stream of hot breath that Tess felt on her face. "I would like to paint all three of you." He looked for a reaction from Tess, who revealed nothing. "I'm thinking of a title," he said as his eyes narrowed. "Body parts."

"Yeah," Vicky said, "I like that. Ménage à trois? Girls only?"

"For now," Wolf said, "for now."

Tess tried to get up and get the hell out of there, but she was so damned stoned she could hardly move. She rocked herself back and then put her hands on her knees and stood, rocking a little back and forth. She shook her head and said, "I'm out of here."

She started toward the door, and Wolf grabbed her by the arm. "Are you sure?"

Tess jerked her arm away and left.

The bonfire had died down to a large heap of embers and ash, and there were only a few people left wandering around in the darkness. A shimmer of moonlight provided enough light for Tess to make it to Handlebar's car, but no one was there. It was going to be a long night, Tess though as she got in the back seat and lay down in the fetal position, a canvas tarp as her blanket.

Just as she was nodding off, Teddy returned to the car. "Hey, Tess," he mumble-slurred as he slipped into the front seat, leaned his head back, and fell directly asleep.

Tess woke at dawn, her body feeling like a knot and her head pinging as though a little man with a hammer were whacking away. Teddy was now draped prone across the front seat, coughing himself awake.

Tess saw Handlebar and William dragging themselves over toward the car, Handlebar with a chain of dandelions around his neck. The two of them looked like a couple of old boys after a hard night on the town—the hair in disarray and the eyes a little foggy, but on each of their lips was a little shit-eating grin.

When Teddy moved to the back seat, and with Handlebar and William in front, Tess got the strongest scent of dope and wine mingled with that sweaty froth of sex, which seemed to be a common aroma around there. Handlebar cranked up the car, took a breath, and said out of the side of his mouth, "Quite a night, quite a night indeed." He looked over at William, who nodded his head and then looked toward the back seat. "Hope you weren't too uncomfortable last night, Tess." He lifted his shoulders and brought his hands up as if to say, "What could I do?" "Those two ladies were mighty persistent."

Before Tess could say anything, Handlebar cut in, "You might say we deflowered those fine women." He reached over and jiggled William's chain of flowers around his head.

William replied in a low, satisfied voice, "And they defiled us."

Everyone in the car broke out laughing, including Tess, who laughed so hard tears streaked her cheek. "You guys," she said, "and your hippy women."

The next couple of days, Tess and Teddy visited a few more Indian pueblos south of Taos. Tess's bracelet received a comment from one Indian woman selling pottery, who looked with a keen eye of appraisal at the bracelet before saying, "Storyteller bracelet has power." Her brown face lifted, and the dark eyes took Tess in with a ken that seemed beyond the here and now. "If it is worn by one who listens and learns."

They took a long hike in Yerba Canyon, and Tess enjoyed not only the rugged alpine scenery but the exhilarating air in the higher altitude. Over the last few days, Tess had hinted around as to what happened at the hippy commune with Teddy and the other Tess.

"I will tell you," Teddy said as he was driving back from hiking at Yerba Canyon, "if you tell me."

"Fair enough," Tess said. She then went on to tell about her evening with Wolf and his female acolytes.

"Damn, Tess," Teddy said, pausing for effect, accompanied by an *I told you so* glance. "That guy was the big bad *wolf*," he said, pausing again this time, waiting for Tess to look at him, "in sheep's clothing." He made a face, eyes emitting a *what the hell* sort of gaze.

"More like a chameleon," Tess said. "One moment, he was the thoughtful, sincere artist, the next, some horny over-the-hill hippy trying to observe and then participate in group sex—his wild, crazy shit." She squinted a look at Teddy as they exited the park road onto the highway back to the campgrounds. "Okay, Teddy boy, your turn."

Teddy lowered the visor as they drove into a strong yellow sun. He shook his head a little and grinned shyly. "I haven't had a lot experience talking about stuff like this," he said as they came up behind a flatbed truck hauling steel cages crammed with chickens. "Especially to a girl."

The flatbed truck was moving at a snail's pace, and Teddy slowly but surely passed that moist, warm barnyard smell of clucking chickens, which infiltrated the van for a moment before the truck was in their rearview mirror.

"What do you want me to tell you, Tess?"

"I don't know," Tess said, knowing very well what she wanted to know.

"It wasn't anything like what we had, Tess." He flipped up the visor as the sun retreated behind a bank of puffy clouds. "After some wine and a joint, it was wham, bam, thank you, ma'am." Teddy puffed out his cheeks, then exhaled. "Afterward ... she got up out of her bed, slipped into her cutoffs, and said, 'Thanks for the fuck.' She then left me there." He shook his head at the memory. "Her name wasn't even Tess. She calls herself that at the commune."

"What was her real name?"

Teddy shrugged and let out a small laugh. "Matilda."

Tess turned to Teddy, her lips quivering. "Matilda?"

Teddy threw his hands off the steering wheel for a moment and looked at Tess, and then the two of them burst out laughing. Teddy began singing, "You'll go a waltzing Matilda with me."

"Oh, Teddy boy," Tess said as she regained her composure, "you did more than waltz."

The following morning on the way to a Laundromat in Taos, Tess said to Teddy, "Let's head west tomorrow. I think it's time."

"I have an old prep school friend living in San Diego." Teddy shot a look at Tess. "'Go west, young man,'" he said with affected bravado. "Do you know who said that?"

"I was a history major," Tess said. "But you should paraphrase Mr. Greeley. Go west, young man and young *woman*, and see what's on down the road."

Back at the campground, Handlebar invited Tess and Teddy to join him and William for a cookout at one of the grills on the property. "William's last night too," Handlebar said. "Seems only appropriate to send you good folks off in style."

Teddy volunteered to bring beer and chips, and Tess to make deviled eggs for an appetizer, if she could use Handlebar's kitchen. "Sure thing," he replied. "I've haven't had deviled eggs since ..." Handlebar looked off for a moment before catching himself. He cleared a sudden catch in his throat and said, "I look forward to them, Tess."

Scratched out on a slip of paper in Handlebar's cupboard, Tess found a recipe titled *Mexican Devils*. She glanced over at Handlebar sitting behind the registration desk and was about to ask and then thought better. She checked the ingredients—chipotle chile pepper, yellow mustard, paprika … and then checked the cabinet. They were all there. Handlebar was trying to act busy, but she could sense that something was on his mind.

As Tess put a pot of water on the stove, she peeked over at Handlebar and decided to take a chance. "How long's it been," Tess said, "since you had deviled eggs?"

Handlebar didn't acknowledge the question for a moment. Finally, he said, "Since my wife, Becky, passed five years ago tomorrow—heart attack. Never knew what hit her."

"Oh, Handlebar," Tess said, "I'm so sorry."

Handlebar came over to the kitchen, his long face etched in sadness, his narrow eyes with a look of remembrance. He stood at the little counter between the two stools, silently noting the recipe on the counter. "Something else happened for the first time since my Becky passed." His gray eyes smiled a soft smile on Tess. "Thank you for taking me and William to the commune." He pursed his lips as if he had more to say and pulled back a stool and sat. "It did me wonders." He raised his eyebrows as though looking to see if it was okay to continue with something that might be a tad risqué.

"Please continue," Tess said as she carefully began spooning the eggs in the pot of boiling water.

"Tantric sex." A look came over Handlebar as though he had surprised himself. "Do you know what that is, Tess?"

"I think so. Healing sex."

"Yes," Handlebar said, nodding. "Those two women brought me and William back to life." He watched as Tess placed the last of a dozen eggs in the water. "It didn't hit me until later, how it had seemed to cleanse some of the demons." He looked up at Tess, seeing if she was still with him.

Tess turned the temperature of the boiling eggs down to low and put a lid on the pot. "I'm learning that life is truly a journey."

"It surely is," Handlebar said in a way to indicate that was all he had to say about his wife and *thank you for listening*.

As the sun peeked behind Taos Mountain, streaking the horizon in a stream of purple and silver clouds, Tess covered one of the picnic tables at the gravel patch with a checkered tablecloth from Handlebar's place. Tonight was her last night in Taos, and part of her was sad to be leaving, and the other ready to see what else the road had to offer her and Teddy. The campground was empty other than the van and William's pickup rig. They had the place all to themselves.

Handlebar brought out a package of hot dogs and platter of burgers he had prepared. "With my own secret recipe—mesquite burgers," he said to Tess as he placed the food over by the grill.

Teddy arrived with the beer, and William came over holding a woven bag, its contents hidden. The bag was intricately woven with a rainbow array of colors in a zigzag pattern. Teddy said not to ask what William had in the bag. "He will show us later. I already asked."

William offered a half smile as if he had a secret.

Everyone took a seat at the table as Teddy handed out beers.

William raised his beer. "To our last night together." Cans were clinked, and then William said, "In a short time, I have made new friends, good friends." He tugged his earlobe as though considering. "The last few days have kept me busy writing in my journal."

"You're keeping a journal?" Teddy said.

"Have been for the last two months, since I began my journey."

"Got a name?" Handlebar asked.

"Highway of Dreams."

"Great title," Tess said. She looked at the three men at the table with her—all from different backgrounds, all so different looking. Teddy with his preppy look and roll-with-the-punches demeanor; Handlebar, a long, lean man recovering from the tragic loss of his wife; and William, the quiet one, the loner, the observer, the native son exploring what was once his ancestors' land.

They had a couple rounds of beer, small talking and gobbling up Tess's deviled eggs. Handlebar didn't comment on them, but Tess saw the glimmer of appreciation in his eyes. William mentioned he had been through the Northwest and down the California coastline and was now heading to the southern states. "Never been there. Curious about it."

Handlebar said he was considering selling the campground. "You folks have inspired me to see this great land."

"That would be good, Handlebar," William said, nodding in agreement. "Remember this though," he said with a dreamy look in his dark eyes, eyes looking for more adventure, "take the road less traveled."

The burgers and dogs were great, especially the mesquite burger that Teddy ate two of. "Best burger ever," Teddy said, washing down his second with a swig of beer.

By dusk, the evening had taken on the end-of-the-day aura as everyone was stuffed with food and drink. William lifted his bag up on the table. "Gifts," he said.

"Oh, William," Tess said, "that's so nice." Handlebar had lit a couple of pillar candles, the faces at the table like ghostly replicas, *doppelgangers*, like the faded wolf in Wolf's painting.

William dug into the bag and brought out a necklace of ruby-colored and dark green beads. Tess was surprised when William handed the beads to Teddy. "This represents a rite of passage."

Teddy put the beads around his neck. "What do you think, Tess?"

"They're beautiful."

"Handlebar," William said, as he reached into the bag and brought out a book and placed it on the table.

Everyone squinted in the fading light to make out the cover, and then all at once it became clear. Everyone roared with laughter, Handlebar pounding the table.

Handlebar brought the book up close and read the title aloud, "*The Ins and Outs of Tantric Sex.*" He shook his head, a big old gapped-tooth smile spread across his face. "William, what can I say."

"Try thank you," Teddy said while still laughing.

When the laughter died down, William removed the last gift. "For Tess," he said. It was a willow hoop with a woven design in the interior in the shape of an eagle, with long gray feathers hanging from the bottom of the hoop.

"Did you make this?" Teddy asked.

"I made everything but Handlebar's book," William said, glancing at the bag. "Weaving and sewing were my way of losing myself in something other than all the problems of being a cop on the rez."

Tess picked up her gift, the cloth material so soft yet strong. The eagle's wings were spread as though ready to launch into flight. She kept looking at it as she ran her fingers over the fabric.

"Say something, Tess," Teddy said.

Tess looked up at William and exchanged looks.

"I see the appreciation in your eyes, Tess," William said. "No words needed."

Tess reached across the table for William's hand and squeezed.

"It's my version of a dreamcatcher," William said.

Chapter 7

TEDDY TO THE RESCUE

The road would offer time for Tess to reflect upon the people and places she had encountered. The past experience stored in her memory bank before fading in the rearview mirror in anticipation of the next. The FBI situation at the Crockford now seemed more like a humorous adventure that would make a great story later on in life. And Jake, whom she had probably never understood, coming from different worlds, each with a different set of rules. Yes, he cadged money from her, but when he had paused after saying, "What if," right before his escape, possibly he was reassessing that if he took her along—an FBI agent had said he always had a female accomplice—he might ruin Tess's life. Maybe he was protecting her from himself. Maybe. Krause, she would always remember that memorable evening, but some of the details would inevitably get lost over time. Handlebar and William, yes, even they would eventually fade, the faces not as clear, the voices a little garbled. But Stacy had never been far from Tess's mind. She wondered what was going on with her and Earl. It had been only two weeks, but it seemed an eternity since she and Teddy had left her at the fairgrounds.

Stacy would have enjoyed Taos. Tess would have given anything to see her reaction and comments about the commune. She would have been on to Wolf right away and let him know where they stood. "I'm on to you and your wild, crazy shit but still want to see what it's all about."

But it was not to be, Tess thought as they pulled out of the campground, William departing earlier in the morning and Handlebar having said his farewell last night at the cookout.

San Diego was almost a thousand-mile drive, and neither felt like grinding that out. William had told them last night to stop in Flagstaff, Arizona, and Handlebar mentioned a campground nearby.

The drive to Flagstaff was uneventful, a stop for gas and lunch at a diner north of Albuquerque. From there, they headed west through the brown desert landscape, mesa and buttes in the distance, the faded sky seeming wrung out by the dry, arid heat.

The Lucky Y Campground was off Route 66. "I used to watch *Route 66* with my older brother," Teddy said as he turned on to the famous highway outside Flagstaff. "Todd and Buzz in their Corvette seeing the good old USA."

"We need to name our trip," Tess said as she took in the high country all around with pine-covered mountains in the distance.

"Well," Teddy said as he pointed to an exit sign for Flagstaff, "let's give it some time, see what else the road has in store before we assign a name."

The city of Flagstaff had a small-town feel, a mixture of adobe and brick buildings with glass storefronts of one and two stories. Like Taos, the place had a western motif but without the prevalent artist community. Some of the people on the sidewalks had a blue-collar look, some of the men in jeans and cowboy boots, the women in blouses and skirts. But there were some older hippy-looking men and women about, with long hair and dressed in cutoffs and sandals. Tess wondered if the landscape and weather didn't draw them to all parts of the Southwest.

Three miles from town, they came to the entrance to the Lazy Y Campground. The campground itself was a wide-open space, similar to Handlebar's with showers and restrooms in a pavilion-type structure, but the rental office–residence was made of pink adobe brick. There were a few RVs and trailers scattered about the property.

The proprietor was a woman in her fifties who had grayish-auburn hair, pale, freckled skin, and the demeanor of a hard-ass cowhand. She had the Old West written all over her face. "Four dollars a night or twenty-five a week." Her tone was no-nonsense and gave the impression of someone who had been through a long, hard ordeal. A widow? The female version of Handlebar but without the personality or survival instincts of life on your own. Someone who hunkered down inside herself and went through the motions, day in and day out.

Tess paid for one night, since they were both anxious to get to San Diego. And it seemed as though this woman was a symbol that it was time for a new horizon.

"The Southwest is great," Teddy said as they parked in a spot at the end of an empty row, ubiquitous mountains looming in the distance over pine-covered terrain, "but it's time for a new view, a new vibe." He wagged his finger as if a great thought had come to him. "We need a view with water. The Pacific Ocean to be exact."

"Right on," Tess said. "What say we treat ourselves to a few beers in town and dinner, and then," Tess said, mimicking Teddy's finger wag, "we turn in early and get our heinies to the great Pacific."

On the road to town, they passed an A-frame building with a sign out front: The Saguaro Tavern. "How'd we miss that on the way in?" Teddy said as he pulled into the gravel lot next to a pickup truck with Brunson's Ranch painted on the door. In the back bed were branding irons, corded rope wound in a tight circle, and an old, worn western saddle.

The tavern had sawdust on the hardwood floor and a few ruddy-faced men at the bar in flannel shirts, jeans, and cowboy hats. A jukebox in a back corner was playing a country western song about a hard-drinking man's heartache. "She done love me for living and hate me for drinking. I'm a hard-drinking cowhand with no thought of remorse. Just another week riding and then drinking it off."

"Let's sit at the bar," Teddy said.

They sat at the end of the bar, and their presence drew the slant-eyed attention of one of the cowboys stationed in the middle of the bar. "Damn," Teddy said under his breath, "it's Friday night, and something tells me them old boys at the bar are gonna be trouble."

Tess started to speak, but Slant Eyes was heading over toward them, those eyes on her. He had jet-black hair, a thick neck, broad shoulders, and a three-day growth of stubble on his dark face. He reminded Tess of a bad guy in a Western.

"Now what can I get the pretty lady to drink?" He adjusted a red bandana around his neck, smiling a crooked smile.

Tess didn't say a word. This guy was scary; his eyes looked like large, dark saucers, and his lips were smacking as though preparing for dinner. Tess reached for Teddy's wrist, and in unison they pushed back their stools—

The cowboy grabbed Tess firmly on her bicep, his grip like a vise. She struggled to breathe as if all the oxygen had deserted her lungs.

"Hey now," the cowboy said in a taunting, slow drawl, "it ain't polite to walk away from a man offering a drink."

In the background, that crazy hard-drinking country western song was blaring away. "She done love me for living and hate me for drinking. I'm a hard-drinking cowhand with no thought of remorse. Just another week riding and then drinking it off."

Teddy said in an even steady-as-you-go voice, "I imagine around these parts, folks don't take too kindly to assault on a woman." He took in the measure of the man, who looked at Teddy like one would an annoying pest. "You don't let go of her now, I'll contact Mr. Brunson."

The mean-ass leer fell from the cowboy's face, the mouth slightly agape. He made a bunched-up face as though Teddy were not playing fairly. He released his grip from Tess as she felt the circulation coming back in her arm.

"Let's go, Tess," Teddy said as he took her by the hand, and they turned and walked out.

Back in the van, Tess took a deep breath as what had just transpired rushed front and center in her mind. During the showdown, she had been in high stress mode, but Teddy seemed so calm and collected. Who knew? He had a vulnerable invulnerability by not challenging with macho visual contact but rather with a look of superior intellect that said, "I'm way ahead of you, and if you cross me, you will pay."

"Let's try dinner in town," Teddy said. "Some place that attracts a more genteel element."

Tess looked at Teddy wearing the necklace William had given him, its beads aglitter like tiny stars caught in a rainbow. She remembered William's word about it representing a rite of passage into manhood. He didn't look so young, his face still had that round boyishness, but there was a look in his eyes as though a switch had been turned on.

"I owe you one, Teddy," Tess said as they exited the parking lot and headed toward town. "But what if a Mr. Brunson didn't own the ranch?"

Teddy glanced at Tess and smiled. "I would've thought of something, Tess. I always do."

Chapter 8

CALIFORNIA DREAMING

They arrived in San Diego in late afternoon. The drive had been uneventful—one diner stop in the Mojave Desert, gas and go. There were places along the way to visit—the Grand Canyon and the Petrified Forest, both of which Tess had visited as a ten-year-old—but Teddy was as anxious as was she for California.

Tess was behind the wheel, driving around San Diego Bay, which teemed with boats of all types, including an aircraft carrier in port. She had never seen such a large anything—it was huge. The water and sky were a rich blue, and everything about California seemed so much brighter and alive than the Southwest. There were palm trees along the bay's edge and skyscrapers across the water and mountains in the distance.

"Chet is from old money back in New England. His family owned a string of mills," Teddy said as he looked over his directions. He told her to exit on the freeway up ahead. "Can't wait to see what his place in La Jolla looks like."

Chet was still at work and had told Teddy to look for the key under a vase in the rock garden in the front. The house was situated on a hillside that looked down on the Pacific Ocean. The interior was glass and shiny metal with long horizontal lines that suggested to Tess a futuristic world. Abstract paintings hung on the walls, broken up in geometric patterns, some bright, eclectic colors, others more earth tones. There was a sterile quality as though it was a model home and had never been lived in. There were no carpets in the one-story home, the teak floors seemingly spit-shined. The balcony—spanning nearly the length of the back—had cushy deck chairs lined in a row.

There were four bedrooms, the master having a sliding glass door to the balcony. Tess was in that room looking down below to an incline that led to the ocean, shimmering blue green from the reflected light of the sun in the western sky. It was so beautiful but also unreal. She felt as though she didn't deserve to be staying in such a place. Was it the architecture, the obvious wealth? She sure hoped Chet wasn't like those rich preppies that hung out at the Crockford, so arrogant and full of themselves. Teddy wasn't, she told herself, and if he was a friend of Teddy, he was probably an okay guy.

Tess found Teddy in the kitchen that flowed from the living room, only a teak bar separating the spaces. The kitchen cabinets were stainless steel, as was the refrigerator. "Some place," Teddy said as he ran his hand over the granite countertop. "What do you think?"

"It's ... very modern, sleek," Tess said. "How did a guy our age get a place like this?"

"It's his great-aunt's," Teddy said as he turned at the sound of the front door opening. "Chet!" Teddy raised his hands over his head and clapped.

Chet was dressed in a blue short-sleeved dress shirt with starched collar, slacks, and penny loafers with no socks. He was of average size, with short brown hair, wire-rim glasses, and a pleasant square face. He had the look of a bookworm and didn't seem to fit in this house of sharp angles.

"Teddy," Chet said, extending his hand.

"Chet, this is Tess Auld. Tess, Chet Lowell." Tess and Chet shook hands.

"Let's sit in the living room and catch up," Chet said.

Chet was doing an internship—"six long days a week"—at an accounting firm in La Jolla and had the house for the summer. His aunt and her younger Euro boyfriend were in the south of France. "Doing her Mediterranean thing." Chet had one semester left to get his MBA at Stanford. He was a soft-spoken guy, but as he and Teddy rehashed some old escapades from their prep school days, Chet seemed to have a party animal lurking beneath the studious exterior. "Hey, tomorrow is Sunday, my only day off," Chet said. "I know a great place on the water where we can have a few drinks and watch the tide roll in."

Can't judge a book by its cover, Tess thought.

Chet drove them in his car, and Tess insisted on sitting in the back. "You two catch up while I take in the scenery." And it was something to see: country manor estates with gatehouses and manicured lawns, private tennis courts, pools, fountains. Some of the estates were similar to the Victorian style of the Hamptons, but others had a Spanish flair with scalloped roofs and stucco. And the air had a fresh, invigorating smell, more so than back east.

The Bungalow Tavern was nestled in a cluster of palm trees overlooking a cove. The inside had a low-key beachy motif with light-wood paneling, a surfboard hanging from the ceiling, and crustacean and tortoise shells tacked on the wall. A round bar was in the center of the space, with wooden booths along the walls, no tables. The bar area opened to a deck with round tables and chairs along the railing. "Let's sit on the deck," Chet said as he waved a hello to the bartender. The crowd was anywhere from early twenties on up, mostly casually dressed, including Chet, who had changed into shorts, sandals, and a T-shirt.

Chet ordered a pitcher of beer.

"A toast," Teddy said, raising his mug.

They clinked glasses, and Teddy said, "To the most spectacular view I have ever seen."

Teddy was right, Tess thought. Small waves rolled gently along the cove's shoreline, and the sun was a large orange orb tottering on the horizon, casting a stream of golden light across the aqua-blue water.

Over beers, Teddy recapped his summer to Chet, from the Crockford on. "Wow," Chet said more than once as Teddy regaled him with details about Jake Langeham, Stacy at the bar in Illinois when the guy grabbed her wrist, Earl, Krause, Wolf, the mean-ass cowboy in the bar. He left out the romantic night with Tess but couldn't help himself when he had said, "Our evening with Krause was magical." He offered Tess a thin smile. "Wouldn't you agree, Tess?"

Tess nodded and only smiled back and then said to Chet, "Tell me about your great-aunt."

"My great-aunt Edith is the family wild child." Chet lifted the empty pitcher toward their waitress stationed at the bar. "Edith Lowell has never worked a day in her life—or been married."

Chet mentioned that his aunt had been around the world. "Many times," he said. "She says she has an incorrigible wanderlust."

The waitress placed a fresh pitcher on the table, and Chet handed her the old one. "She painted all the artwork in the house."

The waitress asked if they were ready to order food, and Chet recommended the burgers. "The best in La Jolla."

After burgers were ordered all around, Teddy said, "How old is your aunt?"

"Seventy-two going on twenty-one." Chet refilled the mugs and said, "She's different, very smart and a lot of fun."

"So," Tess said, "your aunt paints and goes wherever she likes, whenever she likes?"

Chet smiled big and nodded. "Yes, Tess, that is her to a T." He looked at Teddy and back at Tess. "I hope you guys stay for a while. It gets rather lonely in that big piece of modern art by myself."

"I wouldn't mind taking a break from the road," Teddy said. He glanced over at Tess. "What do you think, Tess?"

"Sleep in a bed with the roar of the ocean lulling you asleep." She leaned back as the waitress placed a plate with a small cup of coleslaw crammed between a massive burger and a pile of shoestring potatoes. "Yeah, that would work for me."

They spent Sunday at a nearby beach. Tess took a long walk along the shoreline by herself and then swam in the ocean, the air and water temperature perfect. It felt as though she were peeling off layers of the grit and grime of the road. She then took a nap on the beach, stretched out on a blanket of Chet's. When she awoke, the guys were out in the water, splashing each other and acting like the prep school boys they used to be. Chet wasn't as gregarious as Teddy, subtler with the one-liner quick wit. There was a patience about him as though he had a plan and would take his time in achieving it. But at the same time, he enjoyed drinking a beer and chitchatting about things of little consequence.

When they came in from the ocean, Teddy plopped down on his stomach next to Tess, not bothering to dry himself, while Chet dried himself off and then sat on his towel, looking out at the water. He turned to Tess and said, "Did Teddy ever tell you about the first time we met?"

"No."

"An a-hole jock was giving me a wedgie in the locker room after gym class, and Teddy saved my ass." Chet paused to fake a laugh at his own expense. "His name was ..." He clicked his fingers, trying to remember. "What was that asshole's name?"

"Hayden," Teddy said. "Brock Hayden."

"Yeah," Chet said. "Anyway, Teddy told him to leave me alone."

Tess said, "Teddy boy to the rescue."

"Hayden was a moose, and he released me and turned his full attention to Teddy." Chet shook his head, a remembering smile, and then said in a deep, rumbly voice, "'How about I bother you?' And Teddy just looked at him, his eyes so innocent yet somehow assured." Chet placed his hands behind his back and stretched his legs out, his toes digging into the sand. "Teddy just stood there calm as could be looking at that Neanderthal."

"What did he do?" Tess asked.

Chet brought one leg up into his chest, a hand atop his knee. "A confused, stupid look came over him, as though he didn't know what to do."

Tess looked at Teddy for confirmation.

Teddy sat up. "He walked away." He tapped his temple. "Brains over brawn."

When they returned to the house, there was a silver Rolls Royce in the driveway parked behind the van. "Now it gets interesting," Chet said as he parked his car in the circular drive behind the Rolls.

"Auntie Edith's car?" Teddy asked as all three stopped to inspect the long, elegant vehicle.

"Yep," Chet said.

Inside the car were plush leather seats and a sleek walnut dashboard. There was not a speck of dirt inside or out.

The front door to the house opened, and a man appeared in a dark suit and thin black tie, wearing a flat cap with a herringbone pattern. "Master Chet, so good to see you again." The man had a nasally British accent. His was in his forties, a tall, thin, long-limbed fellow with a pinch of pink adding vitality to his gaunt cheeks. But what drew Tess's attention were his eyes that suggested a willingness to define what must be done and then do it and at the same time maintain a certain contentment with his lot in life.

"Rothschild," Chet said as his face broke into a smile.

Chet made the introductions, Rothschild offering a firm handshake to Teddy and a tip of the cap to Tess before they went into the house, Rothschild holding the door.

Out on the balcony, a woman stood at the railing with a martini glass lodged between her ring and index fingers, with palm up, held off to the side in a casual loose-wrist grip.

She turned at the sound of approaching footsteps. Aunt Edith had silver-gray hair that she wore in a tidy little bun in the back, held together by a dark-wood barrette. She wore blue-gray plaid slacks with a pronounced crease down each pant leg and a purple cashmere sweater over a polo shirt, with the collar up against her neck. Her face was finely structured, with a sweep of high cheekbones, large blue eyes, long eyelashes, and a look about her as though she did not suffer fools. This woman reeked good breeding and old money.

"Aunt Edith," Chet said as he went out on the deck while the rest remained inside, "what a great surprise."

"Chetley, my dear boy. Give your old auntie a proper greeting." Edith raised her chin and puckered her lips, and Chet leaned forward and kissed her. Edith lifted her brow toward Tess and Teddy standing in the wings. "I see we have company." She smiled without showing her teeth and lifted her cupped hand, the other still holding the martini with a speared green olive floating in the half-full glass, and motioned for the guests to come out to the deck.

"Aunt Edith, this is Tess and Teddy."

"Ah," Edith said as she carefully gave first Teddy, and then Tess, the once-over. She took a swallow of her martini and then plucked out the olive, inspected it, and slid it off the toothpick with a dainty bite. "Let us go inside, and Rothschild can prepare cocktails." She cocked her head to the side, her sharp gaze on Tess, a thin smile of appraisal. "You do imbibe a cocktail now and then, my dear?"

"Yes," Tess said, "I would like that."

"Splendid," Edith said as she shifted her gaze to Teddy, who was standing there easy as could be. "Canterbury Prep? Am I right?" She nodded as if answering her own question. "That being the case," she said, offering her hand toward the living room, "let us get to it."

Tess and Teddy sat on a long leather sofa that faced the ocean, and Edith and Chet sat at either end in leather chairs at forty-five-degree angles to their guests and the ocean view.

Rothschild came into the room from the kitchen with a tray of mixed drinks. Tess had ordered a martini—drawing a little nod of approval from Edith—Teddy and Chet, Bloody Marys in tall glasses with a stalk of celery.

Chet asked Edith why she had returned early from Europe.

"Oh," she said with a wave of her hand, "Emilio was a two-timing cad." She took a sip of her martini, dabbed her lips, and took another. "I could not stand to be within one thousand miles of that lecherous lothario. Que será, será." She made a face, which caused her eyes to crease in the corners. But for seventy-two, her skin was remarkably vibrant and smooth. "Anyway," she said in a raised voice in the direction of the kitchen, "Rothschild was getting tired of the Euro scene." Edith's valet and she exchanged glances, each smiling as though, for a moment, they were more old pals than employer and employee.

For the next hour, they talked, or mostly Edith talked, and the rest listened. But Tess found her fascinating. "I bought this house last year, lock, stock, and barrel. I hate the furniture but haven't the time or inclination to change it. It's only furniture after all."

Tess asked her about her artwork on the walls, and Edith went into a long explanation of the various art movements of the twentieth century and their influence on her. "I saw Picasso's work in Paris when I was a girl, and it affected me greatly." Edith looked at Tess as though it was just the two of them in the room. "From that moment on, I knew I must paint."

While Aunt Edith held court, Rothschild was cooking up a storm in the kitchen. From time to time, Tess looked over her shoulder into the kitchen as Rothschild, with sleeves rolled to the elbows, stirred and chopped, seemingly gliding around the kitchen, his long arms reaching atop a cabinet for a bowl while the other hand sautéed onions in a frying pan. The aroma filtered into the living room, a mingling of spices and vegetables and some sort of roast.

After two rounds of drinks, everyone moved into the dining room that was a ninety-degree extension of the living room and accessed to the kitchen by a door-less doorway. Five places were set on the long glass table that held platters of asparagus, brussels sprouts, succotash, a wooden salad bowl teeming with greens, and the main course, a juicy, pink standing rib roast that Rothschild cut, with the precision of a butcher, and served. He then took a seat at the other head of the table facing Edith.

The meal was delicious. Teddy had three helpings of beef, with Edith's encouragement. "Dear boy, I do love to witness a hearty appetite at work."

For dessert, Rothschild served vanilla ice cream with hot fudge sauce, which Edith said was from Switzerland. It was so good. Then tea was served in white china cups, back in the living room, sans Rothschild, who insisted on doing the dishes himself. "Madam," he said to Tess with all the Britishness he could muster, "would not approve of guests doing dishes."

"Darjeeling prolongs the life," Edith declared with the tone of a true believer as she poured a splash of cream from a silver creamer into her tea.

As the sun dipped below the horizon and dusk was settling over the land, Rothschild turned the lights on from a master switch in the kitchen. The lamps, which were silver colored and scalloped and in the shape of seashells, were fastened into the walls by copper rods. They emitted a soft glow of light over the room, and with it, a silence fell over everyone. Finally, Edith said, "The setting of that magnificent sun, down into the depths, brings to my mind something Nabokov wrote." She looked around the room, her expression that of the older, wiser person.

Tess had only seen that expression before on men—old, wise men like her grandfather and uncle. To see it on a woman was a revelation.

When Edith was satisfied that everyone was rapt to what she was about to say, she said, "'Our existence is a brief crack of light between two eternities of darkness.'" She then stood, the queen surveying her court. "Tess, my dear, with whom do you wish to sleep tonight?"

"Myself."

A twinkle flashed in Edith's eyes for a second. "Chetley and Teddy will share a room." With that, she nodded a good night and went off to her room—the master suite with the view of the ocean.

The next few days were spent at the beach, with cocktails in the evening with Aunt Edith and Chet, the shimmering Pacific as a vista. Edith talked about her world travels: "Somerset Maugham's short stories inspired me to see the South Pacific and Far East—by the end, I was as brown as a savage." She traveled by motorcar through South America in the forties: "With the war and all, it seemed the only sensible thing to do. Uruguay was a hidden gem of a place." She pointed to a painting on the wall. It was a male torso with separated body parts floating about in no discernible order.

"That was, and still is for that matter, my impression of a vaquero I met at a ranch on the Pampas." She smiled a naughty-girl smile. "He was the most beautiful of men." She then turned her attention to her nephew. "Chetley, my dear boy," she said as she lifted her gaze to Rothschild preparing dinner in the kitchen, "be a good lad and refresh my beverage." She eyed Tess's and Teddy's drinks. "Drinks all around."

Tess had noticed that when Aunt Edith mentioned her art, a softer side was revealed before she turned back to empress of her domain.

On Thursday evening after dinner, Edith announced that she would like to share her tea in private with Tess on the deck. "Chetley, you and Teddy can talk about whatever young men talk about amongst themselves these days." She raised her brow, her lovely blue eyes offering a look both timid and forbidding.

On the deck, the air was warm but so very comfortable. Even so, Tess had a tad of a chill from swimming for nearly an hour in the ocean. She sat in a deck chair next to Edith, who glanced over at her young companion. "You have a lovely tan, Tess. Savagely so. In the best way of course, darling."

Tess looked down at her arms, and they were a golden, dark brown. She turned the bracelet on her wrist, the turquoise and jade in contrast to her skin.

"May I see your bracelet, dear?"

Tess removed it and handed it to Edith, who held it in her palm, running her index finger along the circumference. "Navajo?"

"Yes. Teddy bought it for me in New Mexico."

Edith continued to run her finger around the rim of the bracelet. She stopped and handed it back to Tess. "You are one of the beautiful creatures—an advantage for a woman, yes indeed, my dear. But," she said in a change voice, a more serious voice, "be careful, for women may hate you, and men most assuredly will lie to you." Edith took Tess's hand in hers and then looked at the water, the sun now below the horizon, the rising moon casting a ribbon of pale light over the water. "I know," Edith said. "I used to be a beautiful creature myself."

"You still are," Tess said.

Edith's eyes glinted a thank-you, and then she tapped Tess's hand to indicate a new topic of discussion. "Would you allow me to paint you?"

The next morning, Edith and Tess were on a stretch of grass on the side of the house. Tess stood with her profile toward the ocean. Per Edith's request, she was dressed in a sleeveless, black leotard that Edith had purchased many years ago. "When I took up the rudiments of ballet during a fling with a beautifully well-formed Russian ballet dancer— Vladimir." The name rolled off her tongue in a musical cadence. Tess liked the idea of Edith painting her, and she liked wearing the leotard—a first. It gave her a sense of freedom, like a black cat on the prowl at night.

"Tess, you don't have to stand so perfectly still," Edith said as she opened her sketchbook. "I want to get the geometry of you on paper, and I will paint it from there onto canvas."

Edith would study Tess for a moment and then draw, look, draw. "I am absorbing your face and body and your spirit."

"May I ask you a question, Aunt Edith?"

"By all means, I welcome it." Edith raised her hand and said, "Please, dear, call me Edith."

Tess offered a little smile. "Any regrets?"

"Oh, of course," Edith said. "But does not every life have regrets?" She was drawing and looking while she talked, her eyes two slits of concentration and the strong, curvaceous jaw jutting out. "If not, then did one even live?"

"Yes, I am learning that," Tess said as a wave, crashing against the boulders along the shoreline, diverted her attention for a moment. "It seems this summer I have learned more about people and have had more regrets than I did in the rest of my life put together."

"Good for you, dear." Edith stopped painting and drew a breath, her gaze on Tess. Her eyes were no longer that of the artist but a friend's eyes. "There is an old saying that is one of my mottos: life is short—art is forever." She motioned to a swinging double-seated chair hanging from a tree limb. "Shall we sit for a moment?"

The chair faced the ocean. There was turbulence in the water from what appeared to be a strong undertow, with waves pounding the rocks.

Shortly after they sat, Rothschild appeared with two glasses of lemonade, lemon wedges on the rim, and straws. He handed out the drinks and asked if there was anything else.

"That will be all, Rothschild."

Tess wondered if Rothschild had been checking periodically on them from the living room, and when he saw them sit, he served them. "What are your other life mottos … Edith," Tess said her name slowly, unsure if it was really okay to be so informal.

"You only live once; may as well die living. That's mine." Edith offered a little cat smile. "And one I heard in India back in the thirties: see the world while you are in it." Edith squeezed her lemon into her drink and then plopped it into the glass. "Those three epigrams, if you will, have kept me going."

The sketch work took most of the morning. When Edith was done, she said, "Come over to the swing, Tess, and see what I have created."

Tess didn't know what to expect: her body broken apart and possibly reconfigured? Her face exaggerated and into a long, nearly unrecognizable oblong shape?

Edith held the sketchbook facedown in her lap, and when her subject was situated next to her, she turned it over and handed it to Tess. A pair of eyes floated high in a pale white sky, looking down at the outline of a woman's shapely torso. A recognizable profile of Tess's head, with flowing windswept hair, floated above the torso. Two bracelets were ringed diagonally and intersecting over the head. A forearm emerged from the side of the body, the hand reaching up for the bracelets. Below and off to each side of the body was a leg with a foot facing inward. There were craggy rocks in the right corner and a shadow in the foreground that faded deeper in the composition. It was as though Edith had looked inside Tess's soul.

"Well, dear?" Edith said.

"I cannot put it into words," Tess said, still focused on the artwork. "But it expresses"—she tapped her fist over her heart—"what's in here. What I feel, how I interpret my world." Tess turned to Edith. "It makes me want to paint."

That afternoon, Rothschild drove everyone in the Rolls to Hotel del Coronado for lunch. It was an enormous wooden beachfront resort built in the late nineteenth century with a Victorian-style hotel surrounded by towers and cabanas around the main hotel, all topped by red-shingled roofs that were in striking contrast to the white siding. On the ride over, Edith had mentioned to Tess that the del Coronado was "Pure Norman architecture, a work of art with feminine ambiance ... I think you will like it, dear."

Edith was right; Tess did like it, very much so. Edith took them on a tour through the main hotel, and it was like walking into a fairy-tale palace: tiled lobby floor, wooden panels, mirrors, chandeliers, magnificent wooden beams and pillars.

They ate outside on a patio with a raised view of the ocean. Of course, Rothschild joined them. Edith insisted that everyone have Bloody Marys. "As an aperitif," she said as she arched her brow with a knowing lift. "I do love how the French legitimize through language every vice known to man."

The lunch was an enjoyable affair, but Edith maintained a more formal manner, as if something were stirring in that formidable mind of hers.

After dessert, Edith took a deliberate sip of her tea, glanced out at the water, and then turned her full attention to the table. "Rothschild and I are off tomorrow," she said with a tone of finality. "I have enjoyed the company of each and every one of you." She reached her hand over to Tess, sitting next to her, and took her hand in hers. "I will miss you especially, my dear."

Tess squeezed her hand back. "And I will miss you, Aunt Edith."

They exchanged knowing glances, glances that seemed to pass beyond the here and now.

Chet and Teddy wanted to go to the Bungalow that evening, but Tess demurred. She needed some time in solitude to digest things. Rothschild and Edith were leaving early in the morning for the Baja Peninsula. "An artist colony is there that I have been told I must experience," Edith had said before turning in for the evening. Before giving Tess a farewell hug, Edith said, "Remember, my dear, 'life is short, art is forever.'"

Tess sat on the deck, her legs stretched out on the deck chair, the night sky aglitter in stars, the moon hidden behind a tumble of clouds, the water blue-black shadows that reminded her of the foreground in Edith's painting of her—*Tess in Flux*.

The sliding glass door opened, and Rothschild came out on the deck. "I wanted to say goodbye to you before I turn in for the night." Rothschild stood there, looking down on Tess, his long body standing so erect and proper.

There was something about his demeanor, the eyes a little sad, the lips puckered as though making a wish. "Would you like to sit for a minute, Rothschild?"

Rothschild raised his eyebrows as though hearing an agreeable suggestion. "Yes, I believe I would." Rothschild stepped around the front of Tess's chair and folded back the extension of his deck chair. He sat with his hands folded on his lap. "I must tell you, Tess, that Madam enjoyed your company immensely." His face was like a shadowy mirage in the muted light from a wall lamp overhead.

"If I may ask," Tess said, "how long have you been with her?"

"Twenty years." Rothschild leaned his head in Tess's direction. "I'll tell you a story if you promise to keep it to yourself."

"I will."

"When Madam first saw me, I was down and out on my luck in North Yorkshire, a seaside village in England." Rothschild raked his fingers through his short-cropped head of thinning hair. "She was staying at a resort hotel, where I was working as a jack-of-all-trades around the property. My fiancée had just left me for another bloke, and I was walking around the grounds like a robotic man. On Madam's third day at the hotel, she approached me and asked if I would like to make some extra money."

Rothschild leaned forward, unfolded his chair, and stretched his legs out so that his feet hung over the edge. "She wanted to paint me." Rothschild lifted his shoulders and offered his hands in front of himself, palms up. "At first I said no." He smiled a thin, knowing smile. "Of course, I was no match for her. Before I knew what was what, she had me in a very skimpy bathing suit lying on the beach—spread-eagle in the sand." Rothschild threw his hands in the air. "Next thing I knew, I was her *jack-of-all-trades*."

"So then, Rothschild is not your real name?"

"Oh no," he replied. "Edward Brown is my Christian name, born in the East End of London—I was Cockney through and through." He hooked an index finger over his other as if starting a list. "She tutored me in diction. 'Don't drop your consonants,' was her constant refrain," he said as the middle finger joined the index. "And of course etiquette, a complete transformation. Eliza Doolittle had nothing on me, you might say." Rothschild slid his legs over to the side of his chair so that he was facing Tess, hands on his knees. "Our relationship is unequal equals."

"Did she ever explain why you?"

"She said it was my eyes." Rothschild folded his arms across his chest and nodded his head a little. "In them, she said she saw competent honesty." Rothschild drew a breath. "She sees things in people that others may miss." He raised his finger as though to make a final point. "She needed a driver and valet." He brought his arm across his waist and rested his elbow on it with fist under chin. "I will never forget her words. 'I sensed you were what I needed—and I what you needed.'"

He scrunched his head down a little and said, "She has been a wonderful employer, if a bit unorthodox."

"That's a perfect description of her," Tess said. "Wonderful and unorthodox."

The house seemed empty without Edith and Rothschild. The paintings on the walls were like ghosts from the past. Tess and Teddy spent the next couple days on the beach while Chet was at work. It felt like been-there, done-that as though it was time to move on, but Teddy was having a blast, and after all he had done for her, she was not going to ask him to take off again.

On Wednesday morning when Tess made her sanitized, weekly call home to her mother to check in, she learned that her older sister, Stevie, wanted her to come visit her outside Kalamazoo, Michigan, where Stevie taught first grade and her husband was a college professor. They had bought an old farmhouse on ten acres.

Tess didn't want to ask Teddy to drive her halfway across the country and back. Plus, she sensed that it was time to break away on her own. She wasn't sure if Edith had influenced this. It had something to do with the painting of her. It was time to get her feet pointing in the right direction and head off on her own. Chet and Teddy were still asleep, and Tess needed to figure out how to get herself to Michigan on her own. She had an idea. She checked the yellow pages, made a call, found the keys to the van, and headed toward San Diego.

When Tess returned to the house, Teddy was out on the patio, at the railing, looking out to sea. Something about his stance, the shoulders a bit hunched, the head off to the side a tad, indicated that his antennae were on alert.

"Hey, Teddy."

He turned, and in his gaze, there was a question. "I saw your note. What's up?"

Tess came over next to Teddy. Large cumulus clouds were steamrolling across the sky like giant, distorted marshmallows in one of Edith's paintings. "My sister in Michigan wants me to come visit."

"Oh."

"I found a company that hires people to drive cars across country—drive-aways they are called."

"Leaving me for good this time," Teddy said as a statement of fact.

Tess slipped her arm around his waist. "You are the best of guys." She took his chin in her hand, his Teddy-boy face trying so hard not to show the hurt. Tess leaned her forehead on his and then kissed him softly on the cheek.

Chapter 9

DOUBLE BACK

Tess said her final farewell to Teddy in the lot of the drive-away company. They exchanged addresses and promised to write to each other in the fall. Then Teddy said something that caught Tess off guard. "Why don't I go with you, and we stop in Vegas and get married?" He said it in a half-kidding manner, but beneath the surface, she knew if she said, "Let's do it," Teddy would go for it.

"Oh, Teddy," Tess said in as light a tone as she could muster. She was about to say something when Teddy cut in.

"Back in Flagstaff, you said we needed to name the road trip." Teddy looked off for a moment and then back at Tess. "It should be a story, your story, Tess. The title of the story should be called *Summer of Tess*. There should be three parts. Part 1 takes place at the Crockford and is titled 'Tess and Stacy'; part 2 is 'Stacy in Absentia'; and part 3"—Teddy placed his hand on the hood of Tess's drive-away, a sleek red Buick Regal—"is yet to be determined."

By late afternoon, Tess had passed Las Vegas and was determined to make good time. It was 2,200 miles to Kalamazoo, and the route went straight through Iowa. But Tess didn't know where Stacy and Earl were; they hadn't spoken since the state fair. Stacy had given her Earl's address, but Tess's gut told her that it wasn't time yet—that she needed to go off on her own for a while and also that Stacy and Earl might need their space together, and an old friend like Tess might be bad timing.

The car rode smoothly, not like Edith's Rolls Royce but much less bumpy than the van, which part of her missed—nestling in the sleeping bag in the back, the musty smell after a rain, and the camaraderie of Stacy and Teddy—but the other part that was growing stronger realized it was time to move on.

Tess drove into the night, and finally somewhere in Utah, she pulled off the interstate to a motel. She didn't feel like spending the money on a room or bothering with checking in and checking out. She parked in the rear of the motel, locked the doors, and opened the windows just a slit, then curled up in the fetal position in the back seat in her sleeping bag.

She was so tired from driving for over twelve hours straight that she was having trouble falling asleep. The road trip jangled in her mind like one of Edith's paintings, everything a jumble of parts: leaving the Crockford in the middle of the night, the VW van in the shape of a yellow beetle, with its spindly legs propelling them forward down the highway; the state fair floating above the ground atop a cloud, the Ferris wheel dangling upside down; Krause dressed in a grey German soldier's field uniform, his large body stretched out, his face twisted in agony; and lastly, Wolf's head in the body of a black wolf, his blond locks draped over his leering eyes.

Tess felt her mind settle as she heard Edith's voice whisper in her ear, "Life is short—art is forever."

The rumble of a heavy engine woke Tess. She felt stiff in her shoulders and legs as she sat up. A semi without a trailer was exiting the parking lot. It looked naked and incomplete without something to tow. The sun was lifting over the horizon, and it came over Tess that she was back in hot-weather country. Her mouth felt like cotton or more precisely peanut butter, which had been her lunch and dinner yesterday.

At the front desk, Tess inquired about a YMCA and was told it was two miles away. She had a membership card that her mother had given her.

After a swim and a shower at the Y, Tess was ready for the road. She stopped at a convenience store and stocked the cooler with Cokes, snacks, and premade sandwiches.

She drove on and on, through the buttes of western Colorado, stopping once for gas and the restroom. The car's air-conditioning made the driving so much easier, as the temperature outside was scorching hot. Then through the Rockies and Denver, past the exit to Buddy's place—he seemed like such a long-ago memory in the rearview mirror.

By dusk, Tess was having trouble keeping her eyes open. She was on the interstate, in the middle of nowhere on the Nebraska prairie, not far from Krause's place. But she couldn't do it. It would be regressing. Why, much like Edith's painting of her, she could not put it into words. But it was there—no looking back. She turned off the next exit that had a sign for a motel for $3.99 a night.

The room was basic, but the bed was firm. She took a shower and went to bed, sleep coming quickly.

Then, up before dawn, she made peanut and jelly sandwiches in the room and checked the road map. She had nearly eight hundred miles left. She had done two thousand in two and half days, and her body was feeling the effects, her back and shoulders achy, her mind fuzzy, but she decided to try to drive straight to her sister's house. Tess promised herself that if she grew too weary, she would stop.

Back on the road, she passed the exit for Kearney, Nebraska, where the van had broken down and Krause, that wonderful man, lived. Tess wondered how the old German and Edith would have gotten along. Both intelligent with curious minds, one an artist, the other someone who appreciated art, but neither seemed to have close friends at this stage of their lives, and maybe they liked it that way.

By noon, Tess had driven nearly four hundred miles, and she felt good, her back and shoulders a little sore, but her mind clear, as though the anticipation of seeing Stevie and her new home were propelling her on.

South of Chicago, Tess hit traffic, slowing at times to a crawl. It was late afternoon, and she had less than two hundred miles, but it seemed an eternity. She ached all over, and a general fatigue wore on her, not that she was going to fall asleep but … she must stay vigilant.

Once out of Chicago, the traffic eased, and after a couple of hours, Tess was a block from Stevie's house as she entered the cozy village of Richland, Michigan, with a common green, stone church and tall steeple, a block of small shops, and a family restaurant. D Avenue was mostly older, modest residences, Stevie's the biggest and grandest.

When Tess pulled into the driveway, a wave of relief came over her.

She had made it. Whew! Three and half days on the road. It was nearly eight o'clock, but it was still light outside. Stevie had mentioned that it stayed light in the summer to almost ten, being on the western edge of the eastern time zone. But Tess wanted nothing more than to crawl into a soft, cushy bed and sleep.

The driveway was along the side of the house, which was a lovely old clapboard A-frame that looked to be in the process of receiving a new coat of white paint, the bottom half not yet finished, a painter's ladder leaning against the house. Tess hadn't told Stevie she was coming. Again, she wasn't sure why that was. She just decided to drive here—que será, será. She went through the gate of a white picket fence, a long stretch of backyard, behind it a field of corn. Tess knocked on the back door but sensed by the stillness that no one was home. She checked the windows, but they were all secure.

Tess went across the street and knocked on a neighbor's door. An elderly woman, with a head of white hair and a round, friendly face, answered with a welcoming smile as if she had known Tess for years.

"Hello, there," the woman said in a warm voice.

"I'm Stevie's sister, Tess, and was wondering if you knew where she and Rob were?"

The woman wagged a finger at Tess. "I knew you were Stevie's sister the moment I laid eyes on you. You look just like her."

Tess was told that Stevie and Rob were out of town for a couple of days, but she had a key. "Great," Tess said, "I'm in luck."

The interior of Stevie's house looked like a construction site. The family room off the kitchen, in the back of the house, had scraps of crown molding in a corner, stacks of drywall in another, the wall studs exposed, electric wire dangling from the ceiling. The dining room and parlor across the front hall were also in various stages of rehab. The kitchen was undisturbed, and Tess made herself a ham and cheese sandwich and washed it down with a glass of cold milk—ah, the little things in life.

She put the dishes in the sink and went up the rickety steps that led to a hallway and three bedrooms, only two of which had beds and only one with linens. Tess didn't want to sleep in her sister and brother-in-law's bed. If it had been only Stevie's, she would have done it. She found linens and pillows in a closet and made the bare bed. Down the hallway was a bathroom with a tub-shower. A good shower before bed would be the last chore before a long night's sleep. She turned on the faucet—and nothing. Tess laughed to herself. *This really is a construction site*, she thought as she headed back down the hallway.

A gentle breeze greeted Tess as she opened the windows in the bedroom, the air relatively cool in comparison to the last few days on the road. The chirp of a cricket and the hoot of an owl let her know that she was in a new environment as she lay in bed with her hands clasped behind her head, her body nestling into the queen bed so very comfortably.

She needed some time to sort things out, as the grind of the road seemed to breathe inside her like some hitchhiker who would not go away. It seemed a blur, all 2,200 miles, as though she had dreamed it and was still in that dream, lying in bed in her sister's house in Richland, Michigan, of all places. Now that she was here, she needed a plan of where to go next, or better yet, how to get anywhere. She had to turn in the drive-away car tomorrow, and then what? It seemed as though she wasn't done yet, that there were more places to go. She needed to give part 3 of her story a title.

The next morning, Tess dropped off the Buick in Kalamazoo, a fifteen-minute ride, and then thought about hitching a ride back to her sister's place but thought better and took a cab back to Stevie's.

She decided to check out an old barn-garage at the end of the driveway. It had a dirt floor and looked creaky and old with a moldy smell permeating the space. There were shelves on walls crammed with paint cans and tools, and scattered about were some old farm implements. In a back corner, a tarp covered something—a car? Tess pulled the cover and discovered a faded green MG convertible. It was a good twenty years old, but the key was in the ignition. She cleared out a path to the driveway and got in the seat. Oh, how neat it felt to sit down low, her hand on the steering wheel. She could see herself driving off, the wind in her face, letting the road take her wherever it may lead.

After a few false starts, the car sputtered to life. Tess drove it into the driveway and let it idle. It sounded good, not that she knew anything about engines. Tess imagined Stacy raising the hood and checking out all the particulars. She could almost hear her voice. "Rev her up, Tess, and let's listen to her purr." Before this trip ended, Tess promised herself to track down her best friend.

While the MG idled, Tess went back into the garage. Behind where the MG had been parked, she found an old, rusty lawn chair and a tent with poles but no stakes. Things were beginning to formulate in her mind—a daredevil trip up north to Michigan's Upper Peninsula. Stevie had been hiking and camping up there and had told Tess that it was beautiful but rugged country.

Scouring around, Tess found a canteen, some tools that she would need, and an old Swiss Army knife on a shelf. Outside, she cut up some tree branches lying about the backyard and carved out stakes.

She turned off the MG, went into the house, and in the front parlor, she found some travel guides stacked on a bookshelf. One caught her eye: "Hiking and Camping the Upper Peninsula." Tess leafed through and stopped when she came to Manistique, Michigan. She liked the sound of it, letting the name roll off her tongue, "Man I Steek." It rhymed with *mystique*. There was a campground in Manistique on Lake Michigan. *Good enough*, she thought.

In a downstairs closet, Tess found a backpack and large canvas storage bag with straps attached—perfect to secure on the back of the car—a first-rate sleeping bag with thick padding, and she borrowed a sweatshirt from her big sister's closet, just like when they were kids. She packed up clothes and gear she would need and left Rob and Stevie a note, and off she went, heading north.

Tess stopped at a grocery store and bought dry goods. Merwin Creek Forest Campground was her destination, 365 miles. It was on a first-come-first-serve basis and provided bathrooms and potable water from a well. What more could a girl ask for?

It seemed different driving the MG after the VW van and then the Buick. It rode low and didn't have as much power as she had expected, but it was a joy to drive, the wind in her face, the sun and sky in full bloom, and the UP in her future.

By the time Tess arrived at Merwin Creek, it was late afternoon. It had been a challenge, but after a few wrong turns and stopping to get directions, she was there. It was all she could have expected. There were picnic areas with tables, stone grills, and groves of pine trees, and nearby was the shoreline of Lake Michigan. The rental office was a large log cabin. Tess parked next to a station wagon with a canoe tied on top, the back gate open, a tent and poles tied together on the ground. The inside of the car was packed with sleeping bags, backpacks, coolers, and cooking utensils.

Inside the rental office, a man in a khaki ranger uniform was behind a counter checking in a family of four. "You'll find the well out back," he said, jerking his finger over his shoulder, "and vault toilets at each end of property." The wife asked what a vault toilet was. "Basically," the ranger said, "it's an outhouse." He smiled and shrugged. "Six and half one, dozen the other."

After the father paid, the family, including a boy around ten and girl around twelve—who looked like she wanted to be anywhere but there—departed, both parents saying hello to Tess.

There were plenty of spots available, and Tess looked over a map of the property and picked one down the lake near the shoreline. "Plenty of good trails for hiking, if you're so inclined," the ranger said.

Back at the MG, Tess removed the canvas bag strapped over the trunk, realigned the straps, and slipped it over her shoulders. She grabbed the backpack, and off she went, looking for Area #10. The ranger had said to follow the trail off to the right and to look for markers on trees indicating a side trail to a campsite. The trail went through woodland of jack pines and deciduous trees, the ground littered with pine needles and moldy leaves. The trees were not especially tall, and Tess figured they were second or third growth. She passed a few markers tacked on trees with arrows pointing to offshoot trails. There was not a sound about, as though she had the forest to herself.

After a couple hundred yards, Tess came to her turn off. The side trail wasn't as worn, weedy shrubs infringing on her shoulders. It was a short walk leading to a clearing and Lake Michigan in all its majesty. Tiny waves lapped the shoreline, the water a dark blue. Tess dropped her load, took off her shoes, and went to the water. She dipped her toe, and it was cold. Noticeably colder than the Pacific Ocean and even more than the Atlantic at the Crockford, but it was swimmable.

Tess set up her campsite, first the tent—four years as a Girl Scout were paying off. Then she unfurled her sleeping bag inside the tent and left all the dry food in the canvas bag. The ranger had told her not to leave any food lying around due to an occasional bear in the neighborhood. "We haven't lost anyone yet," he had said to Tess with a wink. "But better to be safe than sorry."

After setting up camp, Tess went down to the shoreline and didn't see another living soul. She felt so utterly free, as though she had the entire UP to herself. She got out her bathing suit and stripped down right there in front of her tent. Suddenly the urge came over Tess to swim naked. Then she heard the little voice on her shoulder, which had not spoken since the hippy commune, saying that is was smarter to swim with a suit the first time and then consider her birthday suit. Of course, the other voice was chirping right back. "Life is short—go for it."

And go for it she did. Tess ran right into the water and dove in headfirst. Brrr! She began swimming along the shoreline, fifty yards one way and then back. Back and forth she went, feeling stronger as she stroked, feeling alive with vigor.

Out of the water, it dawned on Tess that she had not packed a towel. She got out Stevie's sweatshirt and dried herself, slipped back into her shorts, T-shirt, and sandals.

Sitting in the lawn chair, the lake stretching out to the horizon, an inner tranquility swept over Tess. After a while, she made a peanut butter and honey sandwich, washed it down with water, and that was her day. She turned into her sleeping bag with a good hour of sunlight left.

The next day, Tess packed the backpack with the canteen and sandwiches, looked about the woods, and found a fallen tree branch that she trimmed with her knife for a walking stick. Off she went on a long hike up to Sweeney's Point, which was twelve miles up and back. She meandered along a creek for a while, then along the shoreline and back into the woods, until she came to a peninsula of jagged rocks looming over the lake. Across from Sweeney's Point was a small island, bare save a few scrub trees. Seagulls were floating lazily overhead, squawking. A long canoe came into view, the family that had checked in yesterday, all in life jackets, the mom and dad paddling while the two kids sat in the middle. Tess waved hello.

The parents both waved and offered a hello back. The kids were noncommittal as though unsure of this woman standing there on the rocks above, backpack strapped over her shoulders. She wondered if she didn't look like some sort of wild girl, with her savage tan, her hair a tangled mess, and wearing shorts and a ratty T-shirt. Tess watched the canoe glide by until it disappeared around a bend.

She took off her backpack, sat, and had lunch, her back to a boulder. What a picture she could paint. Behind the little island, a strip of land jutted out into the lake, its dark green foliage glistening in the sunlight, and high overhead, large, puffy clouds lollygagged across a blue sky. Tess had never been so alone, and yet it was a revelation of sorts, Tess in repose. She wondered if her subconscious was taking it all in, and later there would be benefits from this time to herself. What were they? She did not know. *Let it come as it may*, Tess thought as she stood, slung her backpack on, and headed back to camp.

By the time Tess got back to her tent, she had worked up a good sweat, and her legs and shoulders were a bit sore from carrying the weight of the pack for over five hours, but it was all good. Without giving it a second thought, she stripped down and bolted into the water. First impression was that it was colder than yesterday, but oh was it refreshing.

She began swimming along the shoreline, losing herself in the kicks and strokes. Her energy seemed boundless as she glided along the shoreline back and forth. Swimming into shore, she saw the family of four walking along the shoreline collecting shells. *Oh, oh*, Tess thought when they stopped as though waiting to greet her. Tess stopped when her feet could touch the bottom, only her head and bare shoulders showing. "Hi, there," she said.

"Hi, the mother said. "Didn't we see you atop Sweeney's Point?"

"Yes," Tess said, "that was me."

"Wow," the father said, "you must be in great shape."

Tess offered a meek smile and nodded. She was starting to get a chill.

"You coming out?" the boy said.

Tess offered another smile, meeker than the last. "Well ..."

"Are you naked?" The boy's mouth gaped open.

"Timmy," the mother scolded. "Let's finish our walk," she said with a disapproving look at Tess before she extended her hand, finger pointing forward.

They began walking back to where they had come from, the husband turning for one last look before the wife jerked him by the arm. "Robert," she said in a miffed tone. He offered Tess a sheepish smile, and then all four picked up their pace. Tess waited until they were out of sight.

She dried herself with the sweatshirt, her numb fingers patting down her chilled body. She noticed how pale her breasts were—drawn up and rock hard from the cold water—in comparison to her nut-brown torso.

After getting dressed, a pang of hunger gnawed in her stomach. What she wouldn't give for a cheeseburger and fries. But Tess didn't want to venture back into civilization yet. She wanted more time alone, living, breathing, existing. Taking in all around her, remembering Edith's words, "I am absorbing your face and body and your spirit." Tess would absorb the spirit of this great land.

Awaking after her third night of camping, it came over Tess that it was time to leave. She had never experienced such solitude. Yesterday, she had taken another long hike, this one heading in the opposite direction. It was similar to the first, but she ate lunch sitting on a tree stump in a meadow of wildflowers.

She had basically lived on water and peanut butter sandwiches and some wild berries she had picked. Tess felt cleansed on the exterior and interior, as though there were changes taking place below the surface.

By the time Tess arrived back in Richland, Stevie and Rob were home. They had a couple of big news items. "You're going to be an aunt, Tess," Stevie said.

The sisters were sitting at a round wooden table under a weeping willow tree as Rob tended to a vegetable garden at the back of the yard.

"That is so wonderful, Stevie," Tess said.

"Next generation," Stevie said as she reached for a pitcher of tea on the table and refilled both their glasses.

"The other news," Stevie said, sliding a look over to Tess. "Stacy called Mom. She's getting married this Saturday in Iowa and is desperate to get in touch with you."

"What day is it?"

"Thursday."

"I need to get to Iowa," Tess said as she watched Rob trimming foliage on a tall tomato plant with a pair of scissors.

After dinner, burgers on the grill that were great, Tess made a call to the drive-away company. "We don't have anything to Des Moines, only East Coast bound."

Tess realized her trip was in its final stages. "Anything from Des Moines to the Washington, DC, area?"

The man told her there was a car available, but it had to be in Rockville, Maryland, by next Tuesday.

"I'll take it," Tess said, not having a clue how she was going to get to Des Moines.

Stevie mentioned there was a bus terminal in Kalamazoo. Tess called, and there was a bus leaving tomorrow morning at six. Stevie volunteered to drive her to the terminal. The trip was nine hours with one stop in Chicago. Tess then called her mother and got all the pertinent times and locations in regard to Stacy's wedding.

Tess turned in early, things churning inside her. Stevie was six years older than Tess and a full-grown adult. Stevie and Rob had careers in education, a mortgage, and now a child on the way. And here was Tess with no idea of what the future held for her.

Stacy getting married was the clincher. Tess wished she could start the road trip all over again. It had been the journey of her life. She intuited that this was never going to be repeated, that from here on out it was about moving forward and progressing in this life.

She thought about the waitress back in the Hamptons, Beverly, who had the hots for Jake. In her thirties and still not taking the next step forward. Like Stacy said, "Old Bev there, is exhibit A, Professor, as to why this job will only be for the summer." And later, the look of discovery on Stacy's face as she said, "It is the summer of Tess and Stacy—a stepping-stone to bigger and better things." The thought of it brought goose bumps to Tess's arms. Stacy was a once-in-a-lifetime friend, much like this trip, never to be repeated again.

Tess hugged Stevie outside the bus terminal. "You're the best big sister."

Stevie seemed to recognize the uncertainty in Tess. "You'll figure it all out, Tess, not only in Iowa," Stevie said in a calm, even voice, "but after." Her big sister had a knack for offering encouragement at just the right time.

Tess was wearing slacks and a blouse for the bus ride. Something told her that she could meet some creepy characters and best to keep herself covered. She had looked at herself last night in the mirror and was stunned. Never one to be vain about her beauty, but there was a glow about her, the cheeks flushed pink and in lovely contrast to her bronze face, which seemed to have been chiseled. At that moment, Tess wondered if she had reached some physical peak and if it would be a small but sure decline from that point on—or would she hold on to her beauty like Aunt Edith had?

She took a window seat, the bus only half-full, and checked out the passengers as they boarded. They were of all ages, but none would be what one would call well-to-do. For the most part, they seemed like simple folks, whom life had taught a few hard lessons to along the way.

Stevie had packed a brown bag lunch, and after the bus departed Chicago, Tess opened it to find peanut butter and jelly sandwiches. She laughed out loud, drawing the attention of a middle-aged man across the aisle. He had a shifty gaze, sharp features dominated by a beak nose with a bump in its middle, and hair slicked back. He gave off the impression of a down-and-out gambler. "What's the joke?" he said with a laugh, as though they were chums. He slid over to the aisle seat and grinned, as though proud of his tobacco-stained brown teeth. The seat next to Tess was empty, and she feared this greaseball was going to sit next to her.

"Oh, nothing," Tess said, glancing over before reaching for a magazine in the sleeve of the seat in front of her. She pretended to read, with her peripheral vision on her admirer.

"How about some company?" the man said, standing.

Tess raised her arm out like a cop directing traffic. "No." The force of her reply surprised Tess. But it stopped him right in his tracks. He slunk back in his sit, making a sour face as though he had eaten something rotten.

The rest of the trip was uneventful, except Greaseball turning his attention to a middle-aged woman he struck up a conversation with on his way back from the restroom. He then moved back three rows but not before making a face at Tess—the eyes squinting, the big nose tweaked like a snorting pig, and a smug, close-lipped smile—*you had your chance, sweetheart.*

When the bus pulled into the terminal in Des Moines, Tess waited for everyone to depart. From the bus, she watched Greaseball and his new lady friend stroll off together, his arm around her waist. *Better you than me, sister,* Tess thought.

Tess had a phone number to reach Stacy, so after getting her duffel bag, she called the number. A man answered the phone, and Tess identified herself and said she was trying to find Stacy. "Oh," he said in a creaky voice, "the bridesmaid. Stacy's been trying to track you down." There was a pause, and then he said, "Just a moment."

"Tess!" Stacy's voice contained a relieved excitement. "Where are you?"

"The lovely Des Moines bus terminal."

"Hah!" Stacy screamed. "Stay there. We're coming to get you."

Tess started to speak but realized in her excitement that Stacy had hung up the phone. She went outside and waited. Within ten minutes, a car pulled up, and Stacy emerged from the passenger seat and threw her long arms over her head. "Tess! Tess!"

The two girls embraced. Tess could feel the tears well in her eyes as Stacy engulfed her. "God, am I glad you're here," Stacy said as she drew back, holding Tess by the arms. "Christ, you look great, Tess, great."

Earl came over and gave Tess a hug and then picked up her bag, and off they went.

Stacy looked over her shoulder to Tess in the back. "We're on the way to the wedding rehearsal and then the dinner." Stacy shook her head and laughed. "Damn, I could not imagine getting married without you here."

The church was in the small community of Mumford, Iowa, population 465, according to the white placard welcome sign. Cumberland Lutheran Church was at the end of Main Street, a half block of small shops, including a country store.

Inside, Tess was introduced to Earl's family: his mother, two sisters, and father—Earl Sr. who had answered Tess's phone call. The women wore print dresses. They looked tired and worn out, and Tess guessed older looking than their years. Earl's mother looked much older than

Tess's parents, and the two sisters could pass for Tess's mother. Earl Sr. wore black trousers, black shoes, and white socks. Tess thought of the song "Rednecks, White Socks and Blue Ribbon Beer." Also, there was the best man, Earl's best friend from high school, Lamar, and that was it.

Tess wondered where Stacy's family was as the reverend gave a brief description of the various stages of the ceremony. Sitting in the pew behind Stacy, Tess noticed her holding Earl's hand firmly. Stacy was sitting straight up, almost rigid, and Tess sensed a vibration of nerves coming off her.

The run-through took no more than twenty minutes, a simple ceremony for simple folks. Except there was nothing simple about Stacy, and Tess wondered if this small community and the relatives had dampened Stacy's ardor for marriage. It all seemed so rushed. What was the hurry? Stacy was only twenty-two, with her entire life ahead of her. Was she really going to live here?

The dinner was at the home of one of Earl's aunts, a well-maintained A-frame with a large wraparound front porch. The house's exterior was painted beige with light blue trim, and the inside was like going back in time. The parlor had old-fashioned furniture that looked to be from the turn of the century—high-back chairs with ornate scroll work at the end of the armrests, a long divan of similar fashion, and a portrait on the wall of a man in a dark waistcoat and vest, his heavy black eyebrows drawn together over the bridge of his nose, and a stern countenance as though ready to deliver a fire-and-brimstone sermon.

Twenty people crammed into the small space. In front of the fireplace, a folding table, covered by a checkered cloth, had plates of cookies, rolled pastries, and pitchers of iced tea. "Soft drinks," the aunt said, offering her hand toward a cooler at the end of the table. When she spoke, her gaze settled on Tess, as though not quite sure what to make of this young woman. *Another outsider,* her eyes seemed to say.

This was going to be difficult to get through without alcohol, Tess thought, especially for Stacy, who now had a forced smile plastered across her face, as if trying to convince herself this was all so great.

On the ride over, Stacy had told Tess that she would be staying the night with her and Earl at his place. Tess figured by then all of them could use a drink, for Earl didn't seem to being having all that much fun either, smiling when needed, talking when needed, but his eyes gave him away, a look of wanting to escape.

The dinner was actually quite good: baked ham, string beans, mashed potatoes, and apple cobbler for dessert. The dining room was an octagonal-shaped room with high windows and a long oak table running nearly the length of the space.

After the women had cleared the table, Earl Sr. stood and announced, "Time to head home. Got to be at the silo by sunrise." And with that, everyone got up from the table, said goodbye, and left.

Earl's place was a small house, one town over. "I purchased it for a song," he told Tess as they entered the foyer. "Let's go in the backyard and drink a few cold ones." He looked at Tess with a crooked smile. "You look like you could use one, Tess."

"So the hell could I," Stacy said.

Earl waved them to follow and said, "That makes three."

The backyard was a long and wide stretch of grassy weeds with a chain-link fence around the perimeter. Behind it was an empty field. They sat on metal folding chairs.

After a couple of beers and small talk, Earl stood and said, "I will leave you to yourselves to catch up on things." He kissed Stacy on the cheek and then nodded a smile at Tess.

Stacy cracked open two cans of beer and handed Tess one.

Tess waited for Stacy to speak, but she was met by silence.

"Talk to me, Stace."

"Not much to say," Stacy said as she looked up at the sky, the moon a thin sliver. A light from the back porch cast Stacy's face in silhouette, accentuating her strong yet feminine features, the high cheekbones, the determined chin. "I love Earl, Tess, but I don't know if I can live out here in the middle of nowhere."

Tess reached over and put her hand on Stacy's. "I will support you in whatever you do." Something moving in the bushes off to their right caught Tess's attention.

"Rocky the raccoon," Stacy said. "He loves to dive-bomb the neighborhood trash cans."

"Ah," Tess said. "Stace, is anyone from your family coming to the wedding?"

"Nope," she replied a bit too quickly. Stacy shook her head. "My parents don't approve." She shook her head again but with more vigor. "My old man, Scrap-Iron Enright, from Dundalk, Maryland, who got married at nineteen, thinks his daughter is making a big mistake."

Stacy exhaled a deep stream of air. "If I didn't marry Earl, I would be second-guessing myself for the rest of my life." She took a healthy swallow of her beer. "If I marry him and it doesn't work out ..." She shrugged. "Then I will have no second thoughts."

"Sounds like a plan, Stace."

Stacy took a long swallow of her beer, finishing it, and then crushed the can in her hand. She stood as if to indicate a change of topic. "Let me show you my wedding dress."

They went up a set of creaky steps, every tread announcing its displeasure, to an empty spare bedroom next to the one Tess would be sleeping in. Stacy told Tess to open the closet door. There, to Tess's amazement, was a flowing white wedding dress, the likes of which she had never before seen. She reached and touched the fabric. "Is this what I think it is?"

"Toilet paper," Stacy said through a widening grin. "Or terlet paper as we say in Balmer." She turned and looked at Tess, grinning a goofy grin, and they both burst out laughing. "What say we go back outside and get shit-faced?" There was an anxious *let's have fun look* on Stacy face, but beneath the surface was the fact that this was the end of something special—Tess and Stacy.

"I though you would never ask," Tess said, and she locked arms with Stacy. "Lead the way, Madam Terlet Paper."

Stacy stopped and turned. "Whatever happens from here on out, I'll never have another friend like I had with you, Tess. Never."

Chapter 10

END OF THE ROAD

The second day on the road, Tess had less than four hundred miles before reaching Bethesda, Maryland. Yesterday was a long, hard day, not so much the driving but the fact that Stacy was married and living in Iowa. The night before the wedding, Tess and Stacy talked out back for over two hours, reliving their part of the road trip. Tess told Stacy that Teddy named part 2 of the journey "Stacy in Absentia."

"Ah," Stacy said with a catch in her throat, "don't go making me cry."

Tess had filled her in on what she missed, giving the facts and not the essence, not telling about Krause's artwork by her namesake, or the sex with Teddy, or Aunt Edith painting her. She did give a full telling of the hippy commune and all the wild things, but the other deeper-to-the-bone stuff, it would have stung for Stacy to realize all of the bizarre and interesting people she could have met on the road.

The wedding had been a short service with shock and gasps at the sight of Stacy's wedding dress. But she seemed to shrug it off as if she were announcing to one and all in Iowa, "This is who I am." She also was keeping her maiden name. "Imagine that won't go over too well with the womenfolk," Stacy had told Tess.

The reception was held at an American Legion hall, and thankfully they had a bar. Stacy let her hair down and drank and danced up a storm, and Tess shared a few dances with Lamar, the best man, who turned out to be a nice guy who had recently returned from a trip around the world. Tess asked what made him do it, and he said he didn't have an answer until he was in India and an old woman he shared a table with at a restaurant said, "See the world while you are in it." Tess told Lamar that Aunt Edith had told her the same line. "Seems," Lamar said, "that sometimes fate plays an invisible hand."

The morning after the reception, Stacy drove Tess to the drive-away place. Stacy mentioned later in the day that she and Earl were off on an assignment to take photographs for an agricultural journal of soybean crops damaged by chinch bugs in Kansas. In the old days, Tess would have cracked a joke about this, but the expression on Stacy's face deterred any inclination toward humor.

After Tess signed the paperwork and got the keys, she and Stacy hugged and cried.

"I love you, Tess."

"Love you too, Stacy."

After she and Stacy promised to write each other, Tess got in the car, honked, and waved. Stacy appeared in the rearview mirror, looking so small and vulnerable with none of the vibrant life she'd exuded when she'd been dropped off at the state fair, emitting that life force like a geyser of energy.

Tess watched her best friend until she turned a corner and Stacy was gone. It hit Tess hard—it was time to go home. Stacy was married, and it was never going to be the same again. On the road, she tried to think of a title for part 3 of the road trip but drew a blank. After a while, Tess realized that story encompassed more than a road trip; it was about Tess's journey in a formative period in her life. Part 3 would be called "The Beginning."

When Tess pulled into her parents' driveway, there was a young guy about her age up on a ladder painting the house. He was in shorts and shirtless, and even from the rear, she could tell he was handsome. His body moved with supple, graceful movements as he stroked and dipped the brush into a can of paint. He was around six feet tall with a lean, muscular body. He turned at the sound of the car and stepped down from the ladder. Tess got out and said hi.

"You must be Tess," he said. His face had an open, appealing quality. This guy looked true blue. He had a well-formed, sturdy chin, light blue eyes, and wavy brown hair. He was similar in appearance to Buddy, but there was something in his voice that dismissed such qualms. "Your mother has been very anxious about your arrival."

The front door opened, and Tess's mom hurried out. "Tess, you're home." They embraced, and then her mom introduced Tess to the painter. "Tess, this is Will Brockton."

Will nodded a hello, his gaze lingering for a tic on Tess before he climbed back up the ladder.

At the kitchen table, Tess filled her mother in on the wedding, including the wedding dress of toilet paper. Her mother shook her head and laughed. "Stacy is a one-of-a-kind girl."

After catching up on things back home, Tess asked where Will was from.

"He's a boy from Bethesda," her mother said, "studying engineering at Towson State. He wants to teach graphic art design."

Tess and her mother exchanged glances, and something passed between them, an understanding—Mom approved of Will, and so did Tess.

Chapter 11

THE REARVIEW
MIRROR OF LIFE

2008—Joplin, Missouri

Tess was in her studio in the barn loft, stacks of pallets and boxes of painting supplies lying about, shelves packed with paints, brushes, rags, and the like. She was in the middle of a series of paintings, presently working on someone she hadn't seen in thirty years. An email she had received last week had precipitated it. It was from Teddy, whom she had kept in touch with over the years. Teddy had retired a few years back as an attorney for the DA's office in New York City and moved on to private practice.

He had finally reached a settlement on a case he had been working on since he retired from government service. Aunt Edith, who had died three years ago at the age of ninety-nine, had left everything to Rothschild, but Chet's family sued. The final resolution was a clear-cut victory for Rothschild, who retained the house in San Diego, millions in stocks and bonds, and plenty of cash. He was going to open an English pub in Beverly Hills and call it Rothschild's.

The current painting was of Edith, not in the broken-up manner of the subject's artwork but a straightforward painting of that beautiful woman's face. She had begun the series by painting Jake Langeham sitting at bar at the Crockford Inn Tavern, followed by the mellow yellow VW van on the open road; then Tess, Stacy, and Teddy sitting in a booth at the burger joint in Illinois after they felt free and clear, all with looks of joyous anticipation; then Krause sitting in his parlor with a stein of beer in hand, a thoughtful expression across his face; then the hippy commune at night, the bonfire raging and Wolf standing behind Tess with a wolf skin draped over his shoulders. Her last one would be of Stacy in her wedding gown of toilet paper.

In some ways, it seemed like only yesterday that Tess, Stacy, and Teddy had taken the road trip. In other ways, it seemed so long ago. Teddy was married with two kids, one in college, the other graduated. He had a home in Connecticut and another in San Diego, where he lived for two years after law school with Chet and Aunt Edith when she was in town.

Stacy and Earl lasted three years. She moved to New York and was now in the import-export business, traveling the world. She never remarried or had kids and was relocating to London. Tess had not seen her since her wedding, but they did communicate via email.

Two years after Tess met Will, they married. Looking back now, it seemed her subconscious knew he was the right fellow from the start, and once again it proved right. They had been in Joplin for more than twenty years now.

Their two daughters were grown, one married and the other engaged, no grandkids yet. They lived on three acres with two goats, some geese, a black lab, and four cats. They sold the horse after the girls went to college.

Will taught graphic arts at the community college and planned to retire in two years, and he promised Tess that they were going to buy an old VW van and travel cross-country. It would be a different journey, this one with Will, not as crazy as with Stacy walking up boldly to the bar in Illinois—and no Jake Langeham and all the other wild, wonderful times. But Will did promise one thing—they'd have sleeping bags in the back of the van that he would paint a very mellow yellow.

So, two years from now, off they will go, Will and Tess. And somewhere along the way, she will think back on that magical moment in time—the summer of Tess.

Printed in the United States
By Bookmasters